Pirate's Promise

by Laurie Ryan

www.laurieryanauthor.com

tions of this text, other than for review purposes, contact laurie@laurieryanauth or.com

QUALITY CONTROL: We strive to produce error-free books, but even with all the eyes that see the story during the production process, slips get by. So please, if you find a typo or any formatting issues, please let us know at laurie@laurieryana uthor.com so that we may correct it.

Thank you!

Acknowledgements

Publisher's Note

This steamy contemporary romance delivers sharp banter, forbidden attraction, and high-stakes desire where every choice has consequences. Featuring a driven attorney and a wounded pirate bound by grief, secrets, and undeniable chemistry, this novel explores what happens when loyalty collides with longing—and love demands everything.

Set in a coastal village built on second chances, this story is emotional, sensual, and unapologetically bold.

Content Advisory

This novel is intended for mature readers (18+). It contains:

Open-door sexual content

Themes of grief and loss

Emotional conflict and moral dilemmas

From the author:

A NOTE FROM THE AUTHOR:

While writing Stolen Treasures, two secondary characters grabbed hold of my heart and wouldn't let go. Aidan Walker, the fun-loving, bad Irish-speaking agent and friend to Dion Gaetani, and Hawk, aka Hakon Thoralssen II. I knew I had to tell their stories and went back and forth about which one to tell next until I realized who Hawk's heroine would be...his attorney. It made sense for that story to immediately follow his capture. So poor Aidan had to wait a bit. As it turns out, it was a few years before I could complete his story. This re-released version of Pirate's Promise has been updated for current times, but the introduction of the attraction between Aidan and Gail has always been there.

I hope you liked this story and will continue on to the final story in the series, *Dare to Love*. Aidan's story.

DEDICATION

To Christie, who bought my first ever copy of my first ever book.
And to a family that has been more supportive than I ever imagined. Thank you!

PROLOGUE

Off the Baja coast

Three months ago

The small powerboat flew across the swells of the dark, gray-blue water at a breakneck pace, jolting the men with each surge and dip. The tall, golden-haired man stood despite the turbulence. One hand skimmed the wheel housing for balance, his only concession to their speed.

His other hand-held binoculars focused on the target directly ahead, a sailing vessel.

He smiled, much like a cat preparing to pounce. The yacht, single-masted, about forty feet in length and wood rather than fiberglass, appeared to be exactly what he wanted. Collectors loved sleek and expensive. Plus, he could discern no distinguishing characteristics that couldn't be easily disguised for quick resale. A nice bonus.

He saw the family then and watched them play, decked out in their designer clothing. Had they come from a yacht club event? More likely, they dressed this way for every outing.

The blond man shook his head. The sad part was that they'd done nothing but live the insipid lives of the rich. That alone made them the perfect mark for his plans. His free hand tightened into a fist as the shadow of still-raw memories gripped him, and his nostrils flared with a momentary regret.

With a quick jerk of his head, he banished the thoughts. That life was dead to him now. He followed the only option left open.

He plotted the takeover as they approached. They would board before the family noticed. These types made it easy, never considering an attack on the water a possibility. No one ever did. Before long, though, they would know their mistake.

It was perfect. Maybe.

Straightforward, certainly.

But never simple.

His team was well-honed and they were several boats beyond their first capture. God willing, this one wouldn't be their last. Even planned, though, anything could happen. The most dangerous part would be boarding, but his men knew their jobs.

The midday heat, magnified by humidity, blazed into his shoulders. Neither the wind nor the salty spray off the water banished the intensity. It baked the energy out of most people. Not him. He stood taller, basked in the heat, drew it in, and let it energize him. Dressed easy, in shorts, sleeveless T-shirt and sandals, he knew he looked more like a beach bum than a pirate. The smile returned. Even in lawlessness, he was a non-conformist.

He bound his hair back into a tail as they closed on their prey. The action wasn't enough to dispel the acid churning in his stomach. His hand gripped and re-gripped the wind-shield as the adrenaline began to scream through his body. His ears pounded in time with his heart, hammering away, matching the rhythm of the boat as they slowed to a crawl.

Indistinct voices filtered through. He heard their laughter.

Couldn't they hear the approach?

He could. The quiet whine of the engine dying down and the gurgle of water as it slapped the hulls of both boats. Even the seagull that screeched a warning from high above seemed magnified.

Almost alongside now, the oily, acrid fumes of the engine swept forward. His breathing went shallow and ragged as fear and exhilaration fought for control.

The boat maneuvered into place beside the yacht. He used the brief moment to inhale one long, calming breath. His muscles bunched like a lion ready for the kill, preparing for that launch into the unknown.

He didn't wait. He knew his men would follow him as one unit.

The blond man cleared the railing and landed on the yacht's deck. Within seconds, the vessel was secured.

It was over too quickly.

He needed an outlet for the wild adrenaline still coursing through him and let loose with a growl that would have made Tarzan proud.

What a rush!

Feeling very much like his conquering Viking ancestors, Hawk grinned broadly as he approached the captive family.

CHAPTER ONE

San Diego, present day

Swoosh. Clank!

Julia Branholt's head snapped up, and her auburn hair went flying. No matter how many times she came here, or how often she heard them, the sounds still gave her the willies. It was so final. She clicked her heels together as if the action would transport her away. Home, the office, anywhere but here. The life-sucking gray walls didn't help. Neither did the smell. The jail appeared sterile, but one whiff told her it was anything but.

Whoosh. Clank. More distant this time.

Someone was going in. Soon, she'd be inside, too. As she waited for clearance, she reminded herself for the hundredth time that this was part of the job.

It just never seemed to get any easier.

"Empty your pockets, please."

Julia reached into the pocket of her sleek, dark Prada jacket, surprised to find a card there. She flipped it over, and the phone number handwritten on the back under the words "Call me, beautiful" brought a flash of memory. Oh, yes. The Neanderthal from the singles bar her assistant had dragged her to last night. Julia shook her head and slid the card across the counter to the guard.

"Got a garbage can?"

"Yes."

"Toss this in for me, if you would." She would never be that desperate for male company.

"Sure. Purse, please?"

She gave her purse over to the guard. As he tagged it, bagged it and wrote her a receipt, her fingernails tapped the counter lightly, then increased in speed as she mentally reviewed her thoroughly irritating morning.

The meeting with her mentor at the firm had not gone well. Paul Benton broke the news that she'd been passed over for partner again. Of all people, they'd chosen Clive for the promotion.

How could they pick Clive over her? He didn't have her success rate, couldn't even touch her billable hours and rarely, if ever, left the office after her.

There was just no reason.

"Briefcase," the guard said next.

Her briefcase hit the counter with a bang, and she whipped it open. Hell, she'd outdone Clive in spite of the pro bono cases the firm kept throwing at her.

Julia frowned. Like this one that brought her to San Diego County Jail today.

She was fast approaching her self-imposed deadline of partner by age thirty. Her father's portrait, softly lit to gentle the lines of austerity, penetrated her thoughts. Well, maybe not totally self-imposed. Still, she'd made a promise she intended to keep, and time was quickly evaporating. Even more so now that she was stuck defending some modern-day pirate.

Hakon Thoralssen II. What was that name? Norwegian? The papers called him Hawk. The nickname would not serve him well in court, so she made a mental note to remind him to use his legal name. She'd seen photos of the man, of course. No one could avoid them. He'd been plastered all over the television and newspaper for weeks. He rested on every coffee table in the county, including hers. The pictures portrayed a man who didn't look much like a hardened criminal. He stood proud and wore his masculinity with ease.

Even now, the eyes in those grainy pictures tugged at Julia. She'd found herself staring at the photos more times than she cared to admit.

Julia closed her own eyes briefly to right reality.

It seemed like some cosmic fate that she'd been handed the case of a lunatic caught red-handed with stolen yachts. Either fate, or someone at Stanski, Rawlins, and Benton had it out for her.

The guard sifted through the contents of her briefcase, checked something on his computer, and finally handed her a visitor's badge.

"You're cleared to enter, Ms. Branholt."

"Thank you," she muttered with a smile that tried not to say *about time*.

Julia closed her briefcase and waited.

Whoosh.

She crossed the threshold. The door closed behind her.

Clang.

Knowing it was coming didn't help. Julia started at the sound, lost her hold on her briefcase and clawed for it through empty air. The case clattered to the floor, the chaos echoing down the hall.

The latch held. The hinges didn't. Papers scattered everywhere. She threw her hands up.

"Arggghhhhh!"

Could my day be any more screwed up?

Crouching, she stretched to grab all the papers within reach, then did a sort of duck waddle, in her tight skirt, to get the rest.

Real sophisticated, Julia.

A quick glance verified the guard on the other side of the door witnessed the entire event. Crimson heat flooded her face as she stuffed files into what was left of her briefcase and hurried to the next set of doors, only to endure another wait until the guard buzzed her in.

Bzzzzzz.

Whoosh.

And another damn *clang*.

"Miss Branholt?"

She turned to the guard. "Yes?"

"Your client has visitors right now."

"Who?"

"I don't know, Ma'am. I'm sorry, but you'll have to either wait or tell them to leave."

"Damn." She glanced at her watch. Well, she wasn't about to wait. She needed to be in court at one.

"I'll tell them to leave," Julia said.

"That's fine. Room two." He leaned over the microphone and pressed a button. "Hakon Thoralssen—attorney inbound."

"Thank you," she said.

The metal door had a window, and Julia paused before her first real look at the so-called Pirate of San Diego. She froze as instinct pounded away in her ears. The sensation that her life was about to take a drastic turn, and not necessarily for the better, threatened to overwhelm her.

Run, Julia. Don't stop. Don't slow down. And, for God's sake, don't look. Just run.

She placed a clenched hand against the wall and willed her body and mind to relax, her fingers to unwind. Then, she took a deep, shaky breath. And another, calmer one. By the third, she felt back in control and turned to the window.

The attorney/client conference room was a gray, cell-sized rectangle with a door on each end, bisected by a metal table. A chair on each side completed the sparse furnishings.

The face from the newspaper stared back at her in living color. The man she'd been ordered to defend leaned back in one of the chairs, arms crossed, sporting an I'm-on-top-of-the-world grin. And his eyes were filled to the brim with azure charm. Blue like long hidden glacier ice, they drew you in with an almost hypnotic effect.

Julia used the wall for support once again as a trickle of vertigo stole her sense of balance.

Funny. The photographs hadn't made him seem so...massive. The man oozed strength. Two months in a Mexican jail hadn't diminished that. Add in a blond mane of hair and he looked like the MGM lion, larger than life and very dangerous.

Sun-bronzed and all muscled up with a square jaw, light stubble, and eyes—well, never mind the eyes. He really could play the part of a buccaneer. That would not help in the courtroom. Julia made another mental note to discuss a haircut.

She frowned. The man looked arrogant, as if this was just another day, another minor annoyance to take care of. It wasn't the usual state of mind for someone in jail, especially not someone looking at five to ten minimum for grand theft and kidnapping.

Damn it all. She was no coward. Julia straightened, smoothed her jacket and opened the door.

An immediate sense of claustrophobia hit her. Four people was about three too many for this room, especially when Hakon Thoralssen II was one of them.

"Sorry to intrude," she said. "I need to confer with my client." There was no room to maneuver, even though she'd like nothing better than to put her back to her client. It would be better not to look at the man any more than she absolutely had to.

Two visitors, a man and a woman, prepared to leave, which pretty much backed Julia up against the wall.

The woman, almost as tall as Julia, flashed a relaxed smile. "That's okay. We were just heading out."

Hakon Thoralssen spoke then. A deep, mellow bass. A shiver wound its way deliciously through Julia's body. That voice could tame a Tasmanian devil.

That could work in their favor in court. *Mental note: Consider putting client on the stand to plead his own case.*

"Dion and Claire Gaetani," Hakon said, "I believe this is my attorney."

"Julia Branholt," she filled in, since she had yet to be introduced to her client.

"It's nice to meet you," Claire said as the dark-haired man, Dion, helped with her jacket before extending his hand to Julia.

"We won't crowd your time," he said. "This guy"—he tossed a look over his shoulder—"needs all the help he can get."

Julia set her mangled briefcase on the table and slowly took the man's hand. "Gaetani? The same Gaetani who arrested my client?"

"Yes. I'm afraid so."

"I don't think—"

"It's all right," Hakon intercepted. "They didn't come here to discuss the case. They brought me news...good news."

His statement confused Julia even further.

Hawk felt like he'd been gut-punched. His attorney was attractive. Correction. She was I'll-do-anything-you-ask beautiful. And it shot a razor-sharp arrow straight to his groin. He squirmed in his chair, trying to ease a pain long suppressed. He had no intention of going off half-cocked over a pretty face. He clenched his hands underneath the table. Getting his body to go along with his mind was a different story entirely.

Maybe he could ask to be assigned different counsel.

Julia Branholt had a thick mass of auburn hair pulled tightly into a conservative clip at the base of her neck. He wanted to let it down, see if it looked as good free from bonds as he imagined.

On second thought, if she impacted a courtroom like she affected him, he'd be free in no time. He shifted again in his chair. He just needed to keep his pants zipped.

A layer of makeup showed she worked hard to cover a smattering of freckles. And those eyes. No one should have eyes like that. Smoky, dark blue with a kind of clarity, a strong intelligence, behind them. And a lot of ice.

She knew when and how to use them, too. Right now, they seemed to be spitting more fire than ice.

"You're the agent who chased my client across the Pacific Ocean and invaded his home?" Julia asked softly.

Uh oh. Something about her voice warned Hawk not to underestimate her.

"Excuse me," he said, trying to intervene.

She rounded on him, eyes flaring. "As your attorney, Mr. Thoralssen, it is my advice that you not say another word in the presence of this agent."

Oh, yes. She's a tiger.

She whirled on Dion. "You have no right to interrogate my client."

"They weren't interrogating me."

"I'll handle this." Julia cut him off with a slash of her hand.

"Ms. Branholt," Dion started.

"Don't worry. I'll be on the phone with your supervisor before you get to your car. You have exceeded your rights in this case, Agent." Julia pointed to the door. "And you need to leave. Now."

Dion raised his hands in surrender and grinned at Hawk. "I can see you'll be well taken care of," he said as he and his wife walked out the door.

Hell. Did he have to put it that way? Hawk felt heat flood his body as his attention returned to his attorney. His ticked-off tiger brimmed with gorgeousness.

Oh yeah. It's going to be a very long trial.

He leaned back carefully, working hard to feign re-laxation, and watched as his attorney concentrated on straightening the uncooperative documents that stuck out on at least three sides of her briefcase. Her lips were pressed together so tight he couldn't even see the shade of her lipstick. Then her freckles disappeared as skin color began to meld with her blush tone. Finally, she gave up, pulled a legal pad and pen out and shut the case.

"Rough day?" he asked.

"No more than usual. Mr. Thoralssen, we need to talk."

She wore a muted lip color, he noticed. She liked to blend, unlike his Maria, who'd sparkled in all the colors of the rainbow. Just one of the many reasons she'd been loved by so many.

He hung his head as the memory cut a swath through his heart.

"Mr. Thoralssen?"

He straightened. Jail gave him too much time to reminisce. "Call me Hawk."

"What were you thinking, talking to them?"

"Talking to whom?"

"The Gaetanis!" Julia looked like she needed a punching bag to hit.

"You misunderstand the reason for their visit."

"You bet I don't understand. When it comes to your defense, he's the enemy."

"He didn't come here in an official capacity."

"The hell he didn't. He wanted something from you and he didn't seem to have any problem going around legal procedures to get it."

"Julia," Hawk tried again.

"Mr. Thoralssen," she countered.

"Please." His eyes narrowed. "I insist. Call me Hawk."

The tight lips returned.

"Fine. Hawk. You will tie my hands if you give them any information, especially if it's something we can use as a bargaining chip."

Hawk stood then, and the guard outside reached for the door. So he sat back down, leaned forward and lowered his voice, employing Julia's own quiet tactics. "Miss Branholt."

"It's Ms." Julia tried again to straighten the mishmash of papers in her case.

Ah. A career gal. Most likely not married. Or not married enough.

"All right. *Ms.* Branholt, if you will calm down and have a seat, I think I can explain this to your satisfaction."

He didn't know if it was his voice or his use of her proper name that worked, but she sat. It was a start.

"Thank you. Now, as I said, they weren't here in any official capacity," Hawk said. As Julia opened her mouth, he held up a hand. "Hear me out."

Once again, her lips disappeared, and he was momentarily distracted by the memory. Natural lips. Kissable lips.

Damn.

"Dion no longer works for the agency," he said, waiting. He smiled when no outburst was forthcoming, giving her credit for strength and good sense. "He resigned."

Her mouth started moving, and he was almost positive she was gnashing her teeth. His smile widened. He was going to need the tiger in her to get out of this mess.

"Okay. He resigned. But he'll still be testifying?" she finally asked.

"More than likely."

"Then why would he jeopardize the case against you by visiting without going through proper channels?" She used her hands to express her exasperation, turning up slender, dainty wrists.

"I'm trying to tell you." He reached to place a hand over her wrist. Was it his imagination or did her pulse accelerate? "Dion was here to tell me about Tierra Bonita."

"Your village? The one you were trying to rebuild? And the reason you stole those yachts?"

"Exactly. It seems that he and Claire, who, by the way, is his wife now, have been there."

"I got the whole marriage part," she said. "But they might have returned to get more evidence."

"They've taken over my work." Hawk put his forefinger to his own upturned lips before she could put the question out there. "They've continued the rebuilding. That's what they came here to tell me. Dion and Claire have been raising money, as well as overseeing the construction. Tierra Bonita is going to survive, thanks to their efforts. More than that, it will thrive, I now believe."

Joy was not normally a word he would apply to himself, but joyous was exactly what he felt at this moment. His village would live. His home. The shadow invaded his mind once again. It had been her home, also. A lone face filled his sight, beautiful and happy, then terrified and mournful. Maria. A face he would never again see except in his dreams.

"Hawk?"

The soft voice interrupted his reverie, pulling him back to the present. The vision of Maria morphed into Julia Branholt, his hot attorney. His wife's name echoed through his brain, and he clamped a lid on his libido. He would not betray her.

"What?" he said, sullen now.

"You were a long way from here."

"Yes."

She paused. He could tell she wanted to ask more. But she wouldn't. Somehow, he knew her sense of propriety wouldn't let her pry. Glancing down, he realized their positions were different. Instead of his hand over her wrist, her own gentle hands now held his.

"Is there something you'd like to talk about?" she asked.

"No." He pulled his hand away, straightening in his chair. It was time to get back on track. "What do we need to go over, counselor?"

In the corner suite of a Los Angeles tower, Hakon Thoralssen I sat contemplating recent events. The corporate headquarters of Thoralssen Industries occupied nothing less than the best which, in Los Angeles, meant the top three floors of the tallest building in town.

The elder Thoralssen was far from entering his dotage. At a scant sixty-eight years of age, he was white-haired but lean, toned and regularly enjoyed the company of much younger, albeit high-priced, ladies. Courtesans. There were fewer complications that way.

He glanced over to the credenza on the far side of the office, to a small photo of his long-dead wife. Yes, much fewer complications. Although Elizabeth had served her purpose, certainly. The marriage had been a lucrative merger of substantial proportions. In the end, his company almost doubled in size.

Years ago, she'd tried to become his conscience. Now her son seemed poised to take up her cause. Well, he would have none of it.

Tapping his intercom, he buzzed reception. Kate Milden, his new administrative assistant, was fast becoming his right arm. He smiled to himself. At least as far as the legal stuff went. A society girl and the daughter of a fine family, she was tall, blonde, and perfect in all the right places. She'd have been an ideal match for his son.

"Yes, Mr. Thoralssen?"

"Get me the phone number for Stanski, Rawlins and Benton."

"Yes, sir."

She didn't bother him with details or ask why. He liked that about her. In fact, he thought as he watched her walk in with the necessary information a few moments later, there was quite a bit to like. Except she hadn't picked up on his subtle advances. Too bad. It would have been nice to get a taste of what his son was missing out on.

Hawk. He'd heard the nickname. Probably that Mexican whore he'd married had labeled him with it. Why couldn't the boy just flip her for a while and then return to his rightful life?

Hakon Thoralssen I shook his head as the realization struck him, once again, that he did not know his son.

Or what he was capable of.

Reaching over, he picked up his phone and made the call. It was time to plant a seed.

After delivering the requested phone number, Kate Milden returned to her desk just as she was supposed to. She picked up the scrap of paper on which she'd originally written the phone number. The hint of a smile touched her face as she dropped it casually into her purse.

It was another piece of the puzzle. A marginal shake of her head was the only indication she gave that it wasn't nearly enough.

Kate Milden returned to her typing. She couldn't afford to come under suspicion. There was a lot more that needed to be done before this would be over.

CHAPTER TWO

Julia walked into her office late in the afternoon, feeling more like trailer trash than a high-profile attorney. She'd raced from San Diego County Jail to court, barely making her one o'clock hearing, only to find her client, the son of one of the partners, a no-show. She'd done some fancy footwork to keep the court from issuing a bench warrant for the kid. Lunch had been a luxury she, once again, hadn't had time for. To top it off, somewhere during the afternoon, her hairclip had disintegrated. Yes, it had been one hell of a day.

"Tough day?" Gail asked.

Turning to her petite, dark-haired assistant, Julia rolled her eyes. "You wouldn't believe me if I told you."

She deposited her broken down briefcase on the small, square table just inside the door and breathed deeply. She loved this office. Smooth, dark lines and elegant, muted pictures defined the image she chose to portray. It said she'd arrived. Of course, since Clive had been promoted instead of her, she hadn't quite "arrived" yet. She scowled.

Gail followed her in with two coffees and a bagel from her favorite bakery.

"Bless you!" Julia grasped it with both hands, took a grateful sip and set it on her desk, then bit into the bagel.

"Well, I knew you wouldn't eat."

"Who had time?"

Her assistant looked at the cockeyed briefcase, then back at Julia. "You really did have a bad day, didn't you?"

"Yes." She did a very unladylike plop into her chair as Gail took a seat on the other side of the desk.

"Spill it, girlfriend. What happened?" Gail asked.

"You name it. You know, I think the gods are conspiring against me."

"Did you see that hunk of a pirate?" Gail asked, a grin equivalent to a pampered house cat spreading across her face.

Light blue, searing eyes flashed through Julia's mind and sent tiny shockwaves down her spine. She struggled for a stern visage. "Don't call him a hunk. He's a client."

A non-paying and subsequently non-billable one, she thought, but a client, nonetheless.

"Excu-u-u-s-e me, but his picture has been all over the news. His hunkiness is a little hard to miss."

Rubbing her forehead, Julia wondered if there was any graceful way out of this conversation. She opted for distraction as the best defense. "Got any ibuprofen? I've got a monster headache."

While Julia looked over her phone messages, Gail, smile still firmly in place, left and returned with two pills and a glass of water.

"Thank you. What's this message from a Mr. Thoralssen?"

"I don't know. He was mysterious about his reason for calling. Just said he needed to talk to you as soon as possible and that you could reach him at that number day or night."

Julia stared at the message.

"Hey, isn't that the same name as your hunk?"

"You can go now, Gail."

Gail trailed out with a last-laugh, satisfied kind of chuckle, closing the door behind her.

Julia's smile remained after Gail walked out. The woman could be a real pain sometimes, but she was a great assistant. More than that, she was Julia's friend. And her sanity. Especially on days like this.

Hawk came to mind again. She had to admit, at least in the privacy of her own mind, that her client was rather good-looking, in a massive, Herculean sort of way.

Julia reviewed her conversation with Hakon Thoralssen II. Hawk, she corrected. This time, her smile was more contemplative. The name suited him. He certainly didn't look like a Hakon Thoralssen. Much too formal for a... She stopped. Innocent until proven guilty, she reminded herself.

Thoralssen. She looked down at the message again. A father? Hawk had not mentioned any family. Of course, she hadn't asked. Lack of time meant sticking to necessities, so their only discussion had related to his arraignment and some sketchy planning about his defense.

The man wanted to plead not guilty. That meant a trial, and a lot of time, pro gratis, of course. Her boss had assigned her this case because, according to him, she had the best track record with the tough cases. Well, if her track record was that great, why had they passed her over for partner?

Damn it all! Her birthday was in three months. And her goal was sliding out of her fingers like heated molasses. Julia shook her head at what now seemed an impossible feat.

Shaking her head again, she read the phone message once more, then picked up her phone and dialed.

"Hello?"

"Mr. Thoralssen?"

"Who's calling please?"

"This is Julia Branholt with Stanski, Rawlins and Benton. I received a message that you called."

"Ah, yes, Ms. Branholt," the silky male voice said. "Thank you for returning my call so promptly."

"What can I help you with, Mr. Thoralssen?"

"I am calling about your client—my son."

Julia straightened in her chair.

"I'm aware that you can't discuss the case with me, even with the family tie. I just called to...caution you."

Caution me? "About what, Mr. Thoralssen?"

"About my son. He's not what he appears." His voice didn't waver or change inflection. He seemed to be reciting a litany he'd repeated many times. "He's been troubled his entire life, Ms. Branholt. As a father, I tried to raise him right. Boys, however, will find their own way, won't they?"

"I suppose so."

"Well, Hakon has been...difficult ever since his mother passed away. Blames me for some reason or another. Hasn't wanted a thing to do with me ever since. Even went so far as to try to discredit me with my business associates and friends."

He paused, as if gathering his thoughts. "At any rate, that's old history, and all you need to be concerned with is the present. He will lie to you, Ms. Branholt."

"I don't understand," Julia said.

"I know. You don't have any reason to believe me. But be warned. Whatever mission he is currently on, he will do anything and everything to accomplish it, to the exclusion of all else. Mark my words. If you trust him, he will disappoint you."

Julia was quiet for a moment, digesting what the elder Thoralssen told her. "I'm not sure what you are trying to accomplish with this phone call, sir," she finally said.

"You have a good reputation, Ms. Branholt. You're honest, hard-working and have a superb track record."

"You investigated me?" she asked, hackles dancing across the back of her neck like ants.

"Of course I did. I am his father, after all."

Julia heard some commotion in the background.

"I'm sorry, but I have an engagement shortly. I must go. I hope you will heed my advice."

"I'll take what you've told me into consideration, Mr. Thoralssen."

"That's all I ask. Goodnight."

Julia sat for a while after the conversation ended, then buzzed Gail. "Can you get me another cup of coffee, please? It seems like I'm going to be here late. And is there any chance you might be able to order me up a new briefcase?"

"I'm way ahead of you, boss. It will be here before nine a.m. tomorrow."

"You're a godsend. Thank you. Now get out of here and go find your life."

"I'm on my way. Don't work too late."

"Sure," Julia answered automatically, her mind already running.

Accessing the Internet, she typed in Thoralssen Industries. Thousands of hits came up. The first one appeared to be the official site and she clicked on it. She had some research to do.

Two days later, Julia plunked down in her office chair still reeling, fresh from Hawk's arraignment. Things had not gone well. The problem was, she didn't have the slightest idea why. She tossed her mail and messages onto her desk.

She'd tried everything in her legal arsenal to get him released until trial. Every single motion had been shut down.

Overruled.

It had been exceptionally frustrating. Hawk hadn't helped. She had glanced at him several times during the proceedings, expecting him to react. He just sat there like stone. It was as if he already knew how it was going to play out.

The judge had slapped him with bail set at a million dollars! The man didn't have that kind of money. When she'd asked him about approaching his father, the steel in his eyes had gone ice cold.

"Absolutely not," he'd said.

He tied her hands at every turn. Julia drummed her fingernails on the desk. The court ruling today made no sense. Hawk shouldn't be considered a strong flight risk. Even though he'd pled not guilty, he indicated he would make restitution to the yacht owners. Eventually. She should have been able to get him out on bail.

Gail walked in then, the ever-present cups of coffee in her hand. "How'd it go this morning?"

"Not well."

"Uh oh."

"You've got that right. Bail was set at a cool million. Hell, that amount is normally reserved for murderers. Looks like our client will be waiting for trial behind bars."

"So," Gail concluded. "Your pirate remains the captive."

Julia glared at Gail's back as her assistant walked out.

In the next moment, two things occurred simultaneously. Her intercom buzzed just as her office door opened.

"Paul Benton is here to see you, Ms. Branholt," Gail announced as the man sat with comfortable familiarity on the edge of Julia's desk.

Only slightly taller than Julia, her advisor's close-set, narrow eyes gleamed with his own sense of importance. His dark, greased-back hair was never out of place. Hell, it never moved. Slick. That's what everyone in the firm called him, at least behind his back. The nickname worked for more reasons than she could recount. He'd an obvious weakness for the ladies, for one thing. That was too bad, because he also had a very sweet wife.

Keeping her chair firmly in place, Julia looked up at him. "Something I can do for you, Paul?"

He leaned in and placed a hand over hers. "Now, Julia. You're not still sore about Clive's promotion, are you?"

Compressed lips were his only answer as Julia extricated her hand from beneath his and waited. Finally, he shifted off the desk and moved to one of the chairs.

"I came to discuss court this morning. You got shot down pretty hard from what I hear."

"Yes."

"That's unusual. You always manage rapid-fire answers to every curveball thrown at you. What happened?"

"Their answers were faster, I guess."

"You pled him not guilty?"

"His choice, not mine."

"A trial will take a long time and a lot of resources."

"Yes."

"The partners won't be happy. This case is too high profile. You're defending a man who stole from some very prominent people."

"Then why did the firm accept the case?"

Paul glanced out the window behind her. "No one knows. It just showed up with our office listed as counsel of record. The paralegals tried to argue the placement, but to no avail." He looked back then. "The partners want this dealt with quickly and quietly." He paused. "You know, there's been some talk of another promotion."

Julia stared at Paul with the intensity of a fire-breathing dragon. "What are you saying, Paul?" She asked the question with deceptive quietness. "That if I get Mr. Thoralssen to plead guilty and go quietly off to jail, I'll be made partner?"

"Nothing of the sort. I'm just keeping my ear to the ground on your behalf. And action that is in the best interests of the company is always looked on favorably." Paul Benton rose. "Keep it in mind, Julia." He winked at her. "If you need any help with the case, or anything else, feel free to grab me."

After he left, Julia stared out the window for a long time. She needed a distraction and buzzed Gail. "What's on my schedule this afternoon?" she asked.

"You're not going to want to hear your appointments."

Julia groaned. "Please tell me it's not Mrs. Haskins." This was not the distraction she needed.

"Okay. I won't tell you. But if you want to have some billable hours, you'd better meet with her," Gail said, laughing.

Billable hours or not, any appointment with that genteel, southern belle would take an hour at least. She stopped by regularly to beseech Julia to spring her husband. Mr. Haskins, it seemed, had a penchant for moonshine. So much so that he'd manufactured his own still...and his own 'shine. Then he tried to sell it. According to Mrs. Haskins, those "revenuers" showed up and plum stole her husband away, all for a little, tiny bit of spirits.

Of course, Mrs. Haskins regularly forgot that when the police tried to shut down his operation, Mr. Haskins had taken after them with a shotgun. Julia had worked triple time to get the illegal manufacturing charges dropped. But Mr. Haskins had been branded a danger to himself and society and currently enjoyed a private vacation in the local mental health institution.

Mrs. Haskins was lonely without him.

"Yoohoo. Miss Julia? Are you in there?"

The frail voice became more distinct as the office door swung wide, revealing a petite, elderly woman in floral dress, shawl, white gloves and wide-brimmed hat.

Julia was trapped.

Forty-five minutes later, with Mrs. Haskins still bemoaning her own fate and that of Mr. Haskins, Julia's intercom buzzed.

About time!

"I'm sorry to interrupt, Ms. Branholt, but that case file you've been waiting for just arrived."

It was a ruse, a preset code to bring her meeting with Mrs. Haskins to an end.

And about twenty minutes later than agreed on. *I'll get you for that, Gail.*

Her assistant entered with an innocent smile on her face and ushered a still talking Mrs. Haskins out to her limousine. Julia sat back in her chair and stretched. Sometimes, she felt more like a babysitter than an attorney. The cases she'd been assigned lately seemed to be getting wackier. The gods were definitely playing with her.

"That was not nice," Julia said when her assistant returned.

"Billable hours, remember?" The sparkle in Gail's eyes belied the innocence pasted all over her face. "Anyhow, haven't you heard?" She moved to the door. "Patience is a virtue."

That evening, Julia pulled into the curved driveway of her family home for the usual weekly dinner with her mother.

Helen Branholt was in the foyer when Julia let herself in. Sheathed in ivory slacks and sweater and wearing her ever-present pearls, her mother's frail beauty drew everyone around her in. Never one to bemoan her fate, her mother capped off the outfit with a creamy white pair of fingerless wheelchair gloves.

Julia leaned on the arm of the wheelchair to kiss her mother's cheek and thought she looked weaker. The multiple sclerosis was taking its toll much quicker than originally thought.

"Hi, Mother," she said cheerily.

"Hello, darling." Helen reached up to touch her daughter's cheek. "You look tired."

"Nothing a soak in the tub and a glass of wine won't fix. It's been a long week."

"Well, you'll have to wait on the bath, but I think we can manage the wine," she said, patting Julia's hand. "Why don't you go on into the sun room? I just need to check with cook and I'll join you."

Of all the rooms in the mansion, this was Julia's favorite. Airy and filled with plants, wicker furniture and an open floor plan to accommodate her mother's wheelchair, it soothed the soul.

She poured a glass from the bottle of Cabernet that sat decanting and took a grateful sip.

"Ah, good. You found the wine," her mother said as she wheeled in. "Of all the things I've given up, I think I miss wine the most."

"It hasn't been easy, has it, Mom?"

"No," Helen acknowledged. "And it will only get worse."

"Yes. How was your doctor visit?"

"Oh, you know. He said all the usual things. That the disease is progressing, perhaps faster than we thought." A small, quick frown was the only concession she made to the information. "Come now. I'd much rather talk about your week. Why so bad?"

"I have a new client, and it's escalated into a difficult case."

"I heard. The Pirate of San Diego, right?"

"Ugh! I wish everyone would stop calling him that."

"It's what the news calls him. He appears to be quite handsome in the pictures."

Julia's mom-radar went on high alert. "No, Mother. Don't even think about it."

Helen Branholt acted as if she hadn't heard her daughter. "It can't be all bad to have a client for once who is nice to look at."

"He's a client, Mom. Even if I wanted to, I can't date clients, handsome or ugly. You know that."

"Yes, I do," she smiled. "But he won't always be your client."

"He steals yachts for a living!"

"Now, dear. You know the rule. He's innocent until proven guilty. So, you think he's handsome, do you?"

"I didn't say that."

"You inferred it by ignoring my statement."

Julia threw up her hands and laughed. "All right. You win. Sometimes I think you should have been the lawyer instead of Dad. Yes, Hawk is good-looking, in a rugged, massive sort of way. Although, even if he wasn't a client, you know I'm not interested in dating."

"Yes." Her mother frowned. "I do know."

"Clive made partner over me this week, by the way." Julia tried to inject a casual note into the statement, but her mother was a wise woman. She would see through the ruse.

"And that upsets you?"

"Yes. The promotion should be mine."

"Julia, you shouldn't worry so much. You're a good attorney. It will all happen with time."

"I don't have time to waste."

Helen pursed her lips. "This is about that silly promise you made to your father, isn't it?"

Julia stood and walked over to stare out at the flawless garden. Dad always liked everything perfect. The major disappointment of his life had been a daughter born instead of a son. Julia had also been the one to break the family tradition by turning her back on the legal world. He'd died without seeing her graduate from law school. Now, guilt paralyzed her as effectively as her mother's disease.

"A promise is a promise."

"Not if it robs you of life, child. Now come here and sit down. It's long past time you understood just what your father was like."

"I know what he was like. Rigid and unbending."

"And a work-a-holic. Nothing mattered to him except the next case. Not even me." Helen paused as if mulling something over. "Do you know we almost divorced once?"

"No!" Julia's eyes widened. Her mother had never once said anything the least bit negative about her father.

"Yes, we did. Just before that trip we took to France. It was the first time in years that your father took a vacation. And the only reason he did was my ultimatum. It was either go with me or I would leave. It about killed me to say that to him. No matter how much he ignored me for work, I still loved him."

"I'm-I'm sorry, Mother. I never knew."

"You didn't need to."

"Then why now?" Julia asked.

"Because I don't want you to become him. Working to the exclusion of all else. Don't become a bitter, lonely old coun-selor."

Julia sighed. "I won't. I promise." She cringed inwardly. Another promise to be kept.

Helen smiled then, but it was bittersweet. "I may just hold you to that, dear."

Later that night, Julia sat in the study of her condo. Like her office, it was a combination of modern lines and dark wood.

Windowed French doors opened into it from the hallway. Her desk faced a wall filled with diplomas and accolades. In the center, surrounded by all her accomplishments, was a framed picture of her father.

She stared at it now, thinking about what her mother had said. She didn't doubt that they almost divorced. Her father's attitude toward women had always been obvious. She'd spent her childhood trying to make up for being a girl. A's on her report card were looked at with disdain. The all-around trophy in gymnastics was met by some statement about it not being a real sport. Hell, he'd even told her to become a teacher after she'd graduated magna cum laude and gained acceptance into a prestigious law school.

That fight had turned the tables, and Julia rebelled. Turning her back on law school, she'd packed her bags and moved to Hawaii, shacking up with a transient surfer for the better part of a year.

She smiled at the sweet reminiscence. What a fun year. And Mark had taught her a lot about finding joy in simple things.

Then the missive from her mother had arrived.

Your father is gravely ill.

She'd rushed home to find him near death, yet still able to express his profound disappointment in her.

So she made him a promise. She would follow in the family footsteps and become a lawyer. In fact, she would excel at it.

He would be proud of her. He'd smiled then, the first and, as it turned out, only smile she would ever get.

Eight years had passed since her father's death. Julia worked hard to suppress everything she'd learned that summer in Hawaii. Beaches and bonfires had been replaced by courtrooms and briefs.

She opened the case file on her desk.

Hakon Thoralssen II.

Yes, there was always work to be done.

CHAPTER THREE

Three weeks, and Julia still didn't have a defense for Hawk, except for a couple of stopgap measures that might buy time for a miracle. Change of venue would be her first attempt and she had only one more week to prepare for that.

The man was just too damn famous. The Pirate of San Diego. Everyone wanted to interview him and, so far, he'd turned each offer down. Since it was against the law to profit from a crime, payment for an interview was out of the question. Otherwise, Julia knew, he might be tempted. He wouldn't use it for his defense, though. It would get poured into the funding for that village of his.

She closed the file and twirled her chair to gaze out her office window.

How do you defend a man caught in the act of stealing a yacht? Two of them, actually. They weren't his first thefts, either. Only the ones he'd been caught with.

While with the International Marine Bureau, Piracy Division, Dion Gaetani had set up a sting operation, using his own schooner, the *Treasure*, for bait. After a takeover off the coast of Mexico, Dion and his crew were stranded by the pirates. They'd managed to get rescued and track the boat to Hawk's village, where they'd arrested Hawk and his men. The villagers had been dealt with in Mexico and were soon to be released. The yacht owners here in San Diego were the biggest issue. Or rather, their insurance companies. They wanted blood—Hawk's blood.

Julia sighed. It looked like they would get it. He refused to let her broker some sort of deal. The man actually said that this way his village would get even more attention. She didn't have a clue how to defend his not guilty plea.

She'd been to see him twice since the arraignment. Hawk was so damn happy his village would live that he didn't seem troubled at all about his own predicament. How did you defend someone like that?

She shouldn't care. He certainly didn't. But for some reason, this was one case she wanted to win, and badly.

She threw the file to the far corner of her desk, slamming the door on the possible reasons why she wanted the win. Idly picking up her stack of mail, she flipped through it as Gail walked in with coffees.

"Thanks."

Her mail seemed all routine until an international stamp caught her eye. Mexico. Julia frowned. It was addressed to Hawk, in care of her, and with no return address.

"I thought that might interest you," Gail said.

The envelope was open.

"Sorry about that. I slit all the mail open without realizing that one was addressed to your pirate," Gail supplied.

"Stop calling him my pirate." Julia spread the open edges slightly. It was tempting.

Eyes that pierced straight through and a smile that warmed the arctic poles flashed across her mind. Hell, the man even made orange jail scrubs look good.

Julia fingered the letter. She should probably get the letter to Hawk as soon as possible.

"What's on my agenda today?" she asked.

"Not much. You asked me to schedule you some time for the law library. So you don't have anything after your eleven o'clock."

She turned the letter over, then tucked it into her briefcase.

Her one appointment was routine and short and it wasn't yet noon when Julia grabbed her purse and briefcase.

"I'll be out for the afternoon," she said as she passed Gail.

"Going to visit your pirate?"

"I told you not to call him that." Julia stopped and laughed, recognizing the futility of trying to convince Gail otherwise. "Ah, never mind. And yes, I'm going to see my client."

"Okay, but don't forget drinks at eight. We've got a club to check out and hot guys to pick up."

"I'll see you there. But this time, no Neanderthals."

"I need to get out of here." Hawk started to get up, but the guard's pointed stare stilled him.

"What do you mean?" Julia questioned.

"I mean—" He leaned as close as the guard seemed comfortable with. "Just what I said."

Blue eyes focused on her like a beam of light, enhanced by his furrowed brow. His gaze bore into her, intense and...almost feral.

"I have to get out of here."

Sheer will kept Julia from backing away. He was just so big. Hawk in a good mood could intimidate Popeye, and he wasn't currently in a good mood.

"Mr. Thoralssen—"

His eyes narrowed further.

Julia rolled her eyes. "Fine. Hawk. Getting you out of jail is an impossible feat."

"Make it possible."

"I've tried."

"Try again."

"You stole boats worth millions of dollars."

"Yes. And I don't regret one single capture. No one would help. They left me no alternative."

"You kidnapped people and stranded them on deserted islands."

He flinched at the reminder. "We never hurt anyone. Besides, the owners were well recompensed by the insurance companies."

"Yes. And now those companies want your blood. Listen to me. You are detained on one million dollars bail. Do you understand that? One. Million. Dollars. Since you were stealing boats to finance your little village, I'm guessing you can't just write a hefty little check to San Diego County and ask them to forgive your indiscretion. You don't just play a 'get out of jail free' card and walk away. This is serious."

Hawk's eyes flashed, but he didn't move. "Tierra Bonita del Dios." His voice said it all. He was pissed.

Julia swallowed as she fought the instinct to back up. "Wh-what?"

"Tierra Bonita del Dios. The little village you refer to. I'd appreciate it if you called it by name."

He leaned back, and Julia suppressed a sigh of relief. If he wanted to play word games, she'd go along with it. For now.

"Okay. Tierra Bonita del Dios. Beautiful Land of God. Got it." *Damn. I should have read the letter before giving it to him. Whatever it said upset him—a lot.* "What was in the letter, Hawk?"

He didn't answer, just stared at the envelope, turning it over and over. The angry line of his mouth eased, and deep lines of worry replaced it.

That was almost worse. Now she wanted to smooth those lines, follow them across his forehead and erase them. Some part of her wanted to see that king-of-the-world smile of his again.

She could touch him from here. Just a few inches and she could cover his hands with her own, feel again the smoothness that had surprised her. She'd expected sun-toughened skin.

She realized she wanted to touch him, to feel the muscles move and ripple up his arm through those powerful shoulders. Julia started to reach across the table, then shifted abruptly and cupped her cheek instead. She felt like she was on fire.

Oh, this would not do. She could not be attracted to a pirate. Damn. Now Gail had her calling him that. She needed to break the spell she was under and get Hawk back to his usual arrogant self. That man, she could deal with. Sort of. But this one… This one unnerved her worse than usual.

Julia tried for the casual posture Hawk normally adopted. "Come on, Hawk. You can't expect me to help you if I don't know the whole story."

He stared at her. Or through her. He was in another world that only he could see.

"Hawk?"

"Tierra Bonita is in trouble."

That, she hadn't expected. She sat up. "Trouble how?"

"Someone is trying to sabotage the efforts to rebuild."

"How do you know that?"

Hawk crumpled the letter in his fist in answer.

Julia tried again. "Who's the letter from?"

"Dion."

"Dion? The agent who captured you and put you behind bars?"

"Yes."

"How would he know?"

"I told you before. He and Claire have continued my efforts to put Tierra Bonita back on its feet."

"You haven't been here long enough for them to have accomplished much."

"You forget. I was in jail in Mexico for two months while extradition proceedings took place."

Okay. That made sense. Julia frowned. She didn't like this association one bit. "Hawk, that agent is going to have to testify against you. In fact, he's the star witness. You shouldn't have any contact with him at all."

"That's not important."

"It's very important. How do you expect me to mount a defense when you claim the prosecutor's primary witness as a friend?"

"I don't care how it looks."

Julia worried he would tear the letter apart one-handed the way he was crumpling it. She pried it out of his grasp and laid it on the table, trying to smooth out the wrinkles.

Once.

Twice.

Three times she flattened the envelope before speaking.

"You need to start caring, Hawk. If you don't, you're going to spend a lot of time staring at bars."

"I'd spend the rest of my life in prison if it meant safety for Tierra Bonita. That is all that matters." Hawk's hands covered hers on top of the letter.

Julia's train of thought flew out the air vent. She stared at hands that engulfed her own with a gentle touch that belied their size. His skin felt sun-worn, but not overly so.

He was talking again, so she tried to focus on what he said.

"—never begged anyone in my life."

She believed that. Why beg when you can intimidate with a look?

"Not until I tried to help Tierra Bonita. I told myself I was done begging after even that didn't help. But I'm pleading with you now. You've got to get me out of here."

"Why, Hawk? Why is this vill—Tierra Bonita so important to you?"

His eyes wavered, then shifted away from her. He wasn't going to answer. Julia decided to press the issue. She couldn't defend a man with secrets.

"So you want me to help you, a man I've only seen in jail, based on no information. Just your plea?"

Hawk hit the table suddenly and even the guard outside the room jumped. "Yes, damn it!"

Yes? That was his answer? No reason, no life-altering story, just yes? Julia flattened her voice. "Do not try to intimidate me. It won't work."

She hoped.

"Look, Hawk," she softened. "I'm sorry, but it's not enough."

He clenched and unclenched his fists. "Somehow, I didn't think it would be."

The silence lengthened until he slowly got up and started to pace. Two paces from side to side. The guard watched, but didn't stop him.

It was Julia's turn to fidget with the envelope. The urge to read it strengthened as Hawk's distress grew.

Ah, damn it all to hell. He wasn't going to get away without telling her. Julia was his last resort. And if that meant he needed to relive the story...again...well, that was the purgatory that had become his life.

His vision blurred, and he was swept away, swept back to the day that changed his life forever.

Damn it, Maria!

His mind screamed the words. *Leave the boy. Save yourself!* The image grew in his mind. All over again, he saw her running toward him as the black wall descended. She would have cleared it. Instead, she turned away. He heard the sound, too. Miguel. Crying. Too little to sense the danger, the boy only knew something frightened him.

Hawk watched the rerun in his mind with revulsion. A year had passed, but nausea still washed over him at the memories.

Maria turned back, ran to scoop up the little boy, and then both were overtaken by the wall of mud and debris.

He blinked. Facing the wall of the visiting room, he turned and sank down to the floor, dropping his head to his crossed arms and legs.

"My wife was from Tierra Bonita," he finally said, answering Julia's curiosity.

"Your wife?"

"Yes."

She was mercifully silent, and he prayed it would be over, that she would accept it as enough of an answer. He knew, though. Julia was an attorney. She'd ask.

"Was?"

The word was seared in his mind. Was. He *was* a husband. He *was* a lover. His life *was* changed in an instant. He'd refused to answer that question from anyone until now.

"I try not to think about it. It's not easy." He gestured at the walls of the jail. "Especially in here."

"What happened?"

Julia's voice drew him out and, for the first time, he found himself wanting to get it off his chest. "Maria, my wife, was killed during a mudslide after a particularly heavy rainy season. It wiped out two thirds of the village."

"I'm so sorry."

"Don't. Just let me finish and be done with it." He took a deep breath, and tried to calm himself. "It had been raining for weeks. Slowly at first, then increasing to a steady downpour that never went away. It kept coming and coming. Eventually, the hillside east of the village just...gave way." He glanced at

Julia. Funny, in this light, she almost looked like a red-headed version of...

Hawk shook his head and forced himself back to the story. "I heard it, knew it was trouble. I ran to get Maria from our home, to get her to safety. She was already on the move, heading my way. By then I could see the black avalanche of dirt. Oh, God!" he cried. "It claimed everything in its path. She could have reached me. Hell, she was so close I could see the expression on her face. I was this close." Hawk snapped his fingers together. "Almost close enough to pull her out of harm's way, damn it. I heard the sound then. A child's wail. I knew the exact moment when she heard it, too. We both turned and saw Miguel, standing on his porch, in the path of the mud. One last glance. That's all I got. Then, she swerved and turned away from me, toward him." He stared at the floor. "The wall of mud swallowed them both."

"You—"

He cut her off. He didn't want the ugliness to come from her mouth. "Yes. I watched them both die. I tried to get to her even after the mudflow stilled, but it was like quicksand. Then the others in my village pulled me back."

Julia watched in horror as her mind's eye brought his words to life. He was a roaring lion, insane with grief and fear, tossing men every which way to get free, to save his mate.

"How can I help?" she asked.

Hawk rose and returned to the table. A small spark of his arrogance returned as he sat down.

"It's simple. Bail me out."

"Simple. Right. Just bail you out. Never mind that I don't have that kind of money, or that it's unethical. I could get disbarred."

"Then find another way," he said.

Julia began to drum her fingers on the table as she searched for any solution. There was only one that she could come up with.

"Your father called me."

Hawk stiffened. "What did that bastard want?"

"He warned me about you."

"I can just bet," he spat.

"Hawk, I think you need to ask your father for help."

"Absolutely not."

Julia threw her hands up in the air. "Why not?"

"Because I said so. Because that bastard wrote me off when I wouldn't play his underhanded games of subterfuge." Hawk shook his head. "Because I refuse to be pulled back into that duplicitous society."

Stubborn fool. "I don't have any other ideas."

"Think of one."

"I'll try, but if you had trouble acquiring funds for your village, what makes you think we can come up with bail?"

"Just get me out of here, Julia. Please. I'm begging you."

"I—"

"Promise me you'll try."

Another promise. She knew full well the weight tied to promises. It plunked you from the beach and chained you to a desk. It sucked any desire for a life beyond work right out of your soul. It ate away at your will until there was nothing left.

"You don't know what you're asking."

"I'm sorry. I've got no one else to ask."

Elbows on the table, Julia rubbed her temples, which had begun to pound out a beat. "I honestly don't think it's possible," she said in a voice meant only for her.

"Please." With his hand under her chin, he tipped her head up.

The feeling of being slowly crushed between two opposing walls threatened to overwhelm her, and she took a deep, ragged breath before answering. "All right. I-I promise."

Hawk's voice was barely audible. "Thank you."

She left him, enduring another set of the *whoosh, clang* of the jail doors and, at last, freedom. As she breathed in the San Diego winter air, Julia pulled her jacket close.

She'd relocated here five years ago. Her first winter, she'd worn short sleeve shirts and wondered why everyone felt so cold. Acclimated now, the sixty degree weather was cool and bordered on crisp. Still, it wasn't just the temperature that had her shivering. She hurried to her car, certain she would not be able to resolve Hawk's dilemma, and equally as certain that she would have to make a decision between the pledge to her father and the one to Hawk. One would destroy the other.

Altitudes Sky Lounge was crazy busy. At least Gail had managed to snag a table. Colored panels and low lighting made it hard to tell for sure, but it appeared to be standing room only. If the guy behind her jostled her one more time as he gesticulated over some story or pick-up line, Julia was going to get nasty.

She took a sip of her drink and went squidgy-eyed in response to the sweet tartness. Swirling the maroon-colored liquid, she tried to place the flavor but couldn't. She leaned across the table to be heard over the DJ's current choice for meet-and-greet music. Personally, she didn't understand how much "greeting" could occur at this decibel level.

"What is this?" she asked Gail.

"It's a pomtini. Pomegranates. It's the latest rage."

Julia pushed it away. She'd rage about it, all right.

"Oh my gosh, this place is hopping," Gail said.

"Yes, it—oomph!" The guy behind her backed up and bumped her half off her stool.

Putting a little more force into it than she planned, she elbowed him. At the same moment he turned her way and, since he was standing, she caught him right in the groin.

"Oh, my God," Julia said, covering her mouth to hide the laugh that wouldn't quite go away. This night was going from bad to worse. "I'm so sorry."

"Mmmmm," he groaned. "That's okay. I think I'll live."

He straightened, then took a long moment to give Julia a once over that had her wishing for a shower. To her absolute amazement, he turned Mr. Charm on.

"No harm done," he said, placing a hand on the back of her bar chair. "So, don't I know you from somewhere?"

She rolled her eyes at Gail, who watched with rapt fascination. How was it that friends thought they knew what you needed better than you did?

Julia turned back to tall, dark, and obnoxious. "I don't think so."

"You're probably right." He leaned in and twirled an auburn strand of her hair in his fingers. "I'd definitely remember you."

Pulling the hair out of his fingers, she turned on her sexiest, sultriest voice. "On second thought, maybe I do remember you."

He grinned and his hand started to caress her back.

Suppressing the urge to shudder, she raised her voice a notch. "Aren't you the perp I put behind bars for looking at child pornography a few months ago?"

The look on his face was priceless. Widened eyes and an open mouth gave way to a hurried glance about to see if anyone else heard. Then he turned back toward her. "I don't know who the hell you're talking about, lady, but it damn sure wasn't me." He stalked off into the night and Julia breathed a sigh of relief.

The pained look on Gail's face said it all. "You could have at least given him a chance, you know."

"Oh, please. He's a player. And a bad one, at that."

"Hey, at least he's out here trying, instead of using work as an excuse to avoid having a life."

Julia started to retort, but what could she say? Gail was right. It was all about the job right now. "I'll have a life one of these days," she said, placing a hand over her friend's. "For now, though, this is the way it has to be."

"Well, don't wait too long, okay? After all, you're not getting any younger."

"Ouch," Julia said, seeing the jest in Gail's wide grin.

"You may not want to play, but I do. I'm going to go mingle. You okay here?"

"I'm fine," Julia said, waving a hand. "Go. Have fun. Be safe."

Julia watched her friend wander off, and wondered why she didn't have the flirting gene. This kind of pick-me-up small talk was beyond her.

A partner would be nice. Hell, sex would be even better. Not one to flop with casual partners, she missed sex. She looked around the lounge, aware that the type of man she'd like to meet wouldn't be caught dead in a place like this. She needed someone who believed in commitment, but had a good sense of humor. Someone who made her smile each time she saw him, with his long, blond mane and a body that inflamed her senses.

Julia propped her head in her hand, staring at the multi-colored light panels without seeing them.

She needed someone like Hawk.

She sat up. Hawk?

No way. The man was a walking disaster. He was in jail. And her client. He was...

A pain in the ass. One she had no intention of getting involved with beyond getting him out of jail.

She sighed, any lingering desire to be in a lounge gone. Grabbing her purse, she found Gail, along with several other women, surrounding some dark Adonis. Judging by the attention he was giving her, Julia doubted Gail would be lonely tonight.

Two days later, Julia pulled into the parking lot of San Diego County Jail as clueless as when she'd last seen Hawk. He was her client, for God's sake. There was no legal way for her to get him out of jail, except to find someone to post bond. He'd closed the door on his father, the one person who had the financial ability to do that.

She rested her head on the steering wheel, dreading this meeting. She'd researched the village, finding precious little on the Internet. Only a couple of brief stories in a Mexican newspaper about the mudslide, probably because of the nine deaths attributed to it. One of them was Maria Thoralssen, Hawk's wife.

One million dollars bail. Even at the ten percent that bail bondsmen wanted, that meant one hundred thousand dollars. She'd tried that avenue. They didn't want to touch it for anything less than thirty percent. They thought her client was a flight risk.

Julia shook her head. They were right.

Now she needed to tell Hawk the bad news. She hadn't come up with any way to free him. There was only one option left, and he wasn't going to like it.

"Well," she said, "guess it's time to get this over with." She stepped out, straightened her suit, reached for her briefcase and entered the jail.

Whoosh. Clank.

She walked up to the guard. "I'd like to see Hakon Thoralssen, please."

"I'm sorry, miss," the man said without even a glance at his monitor. "Hakon Thoralssen is no longer here."

CHAPTER FOUR

"What do you mean, he's not here?" Julia drummed her fingers on the jail counter.

"Hakon Thoralssen was released, Ms. Branholt," the guard answered.

Her fingers stopped mid-tap. "Released? When?"

"You probably passed him on your way in."

She thought of the blond giant and felt the warmth creeping into her cheeks. No, she'd definitely remember if she'd seen him.

"How could he get released? Bail is one million dollars. The man doesn't have that kind of money." If he did, he wouldn't be in this mess.

"A bond was posted for bail."

"By whom?"

The guard checked his computer screen, then glanced up with an odd look on his face.

"According to the records, Ms. Branholt, you did."

"Me?" Stunned, Julia stared at the man.

"Yes, ma'am. That's what it says."

She felt the color drain from her face. "It can't say that." She reached to turn the computer screen, but the guard's outstretched hand stopped her. "This is ridiculous. Why would I be here if I posted bail? It can't list me. Check again, please."

"I'm sorry, but that won't change what it says."

"How in the hell could I have posted bond? I've been in court all morning." She started tapping her nails again, faster now.

"It says here bond was posted through an agency by courier," the guard said.

"But I—" Julia stopped. Arguing with the guard was useless. He could only read what was in front of him. Someone posted bail for Hawk. And somehow, her name had been attached to it.

The headache that had begun to take hold in the car stepped up its assault and Julia rubbed her forehead.

This was an ethics issue of monumental proportions. She could be disbarred for helping a client this way. Even being associated with the attempt could mean censure. How could this have happened?

Julia straightened. The question wasn't how. It should be who. Someone posted bail in her name. Someone freed Hawk and screwed her career in one simple maneuver. Did Hawk pull somebody out of the woodwork? She couldn't believe that he would intentionally put her career at risk. Or that he had the kind of friends that could help him like this. Still, it must be someone he knew. Or...someone who knew about him.

She slammed her fists on the counter. She was damn sure going to find out who had done this, as well as how they managed to drag her into this mess.

She looked at the guard. "I need a copy of the bail forms."

"You'll have to go to Records down the hall to put in a request."

"Fine," she answered through tight lips. "Can you at least tell me the name of the bond company?"

"Yes, ma'am. Sure Deal Bail Bonds."

She didn't know them. Not that she had much experience with bondsmen. She worked mostly high-end cases. Posting bond was generally not an issue. Julia grabbed her briefcase and turned on her heel with a quick "thank you" tossed over her shoulder.

The stone wall of bureaucracy in Records stole the last bit of patience she had left. After filling out the forms and being told it would take two to three days to process, Julia left county lock-up feeling numb.

This was absurd! She didn't have access to the kind of money it took to bail Hawk out.

Julia froze twenty yards from her car. However it happened, her name was listed as posting bail for her own client. Damn it. If the partners got a hold of this…

"Thanks for the freedom, counselor."

Julia's mid-air pirouette would have done a cat proud. "Hawk!"

There, in all his golden glory, stood Hakon Thoralssen II. No table between them. No guards. No nothing, except a lion who appeared taller, broader and more dangerous than ever.

She took a step back, then another as he smiled.

"At your service, ma'am."

All it took was a smile and he went from fierce feline to trust-me handsome. Julia's heart betrayed her and raced to fill her cheeks with warmth as everything started to move in slow motion.

He tucked his hands in his back pockets, and her body tingled as she wondered how those hands would feel roaming across her. A heat burned deep inside her, expanding so rapidly she could not suppress it.

She tried.

He is my client. Then, she saw the breeze lightly rustle his blond hair and barely caught herself before she reached up to run her hands through it.

He is my client.

Hawk swallowed, and she couldn't tear her eyes away from the power of neck muscles honed to perfection. A glance upward revealed eyes glowing with pleasure. Eyes that said "come hither" underlined by shadows that said "grieving widower."

He is my client. And he is still married to his dead wife.

That worked. Julia dug deep to find her voice. "How did you get here?"

He closed the distance between them conspiratorially. "I have many talents, counselor."

Julia's throat started to constrict and she fought to keep herself from gulping air. She backed up until she was against her car.

He followed.

He was too close. That boyish grin of his wasn't doing a damn thing to calm her. She needed to dredge up some righteous anger. And some space.

"Back off, Mr. Thoralssen."

Hawk moved in closer. "Call me Hawk."

"F-fine." Damn. She'd taken on ferocious opponents in court and here she was, quavering like a jellyfish. Time to get back in control. "Back off, Hawk."

He did, just enough to allow her a deep breath. She closed her eyes, willing her desire to dissipate.

"Worried, counselor?"

For all the wrong reasons. "Not at all," she lied. "What are you doing here? I figured you'd be long gone by now."

That did the trick. Hawk gave her more space and ran his fingers through his hair.

Julia stood spellbound.

"I just wanted to thank you," Hawk said.

"Me? For what?"

"For my freedom. I don't know how you did it, but I'm out of jail and grateful to you."

She shook her head. "I didn't."

"Didn't what?"

"Didn't do a damn thing. I didn't bail you out. So you tell me, Hawk. Just who the hell did?"

The intensity of his need to be closer to her hit Hawk like a tsunami. The fact that Julia hadn't bailed him out was the concrete dam that stopped the storm. Stunned, he turned and leaned against the car next to her.

"The guard said you posted bail."

"Once again, I did not."

"Who, then?"

"That's what I would like very much to know. And I'm in a lot of trouble if I don't find out. Soon."

"Trouble how?"

She gave him one of those do-I-have-to-spell-it-out-for-you expressions. He barely saw it. Even filled with cold anger as they were now, her dark blue eyes made his heart race like molten lava.

"An attorney can help a client only so far. As soon as there is any resemblance to a personal stake in the case, a line has been crossed. An ethical line. Posting bond is considered a personal infringement in any case." She gazed out over the parking lot. "It could mean being barred from practicing law."

His gut felt like he'd just gone twenty rounds with Muhammad Ali. He didn't want this to happen to her. Hell, he didn't want her involved at all. Now, it appeared, she was being pulled into his problems against her will, and there wasn't a damn thing he could do about it. He had other priorities.

Shit.

"I'm sorry," he said, knowing it wouldn't help.

"So am I."

He turned to her, well aware she would not like what he was about to say. "You remember the letter I got from Dion, right?"

"Yes."

"Someone is sabotaging the village."

"I remember." Julia jammed her hands into her jacket pockets.

"I would have to guess that whoever is doing that is also messing with us—with you."

"Any idea who that could be?"

Hawk grimaced. "Not a clue."

"All right. Then how do we find out?"

"I can't help with this. Not right now. I have to go home."

"Home?" She turned to him, hands out of pockets and firmly placed on her hips. "You mean, to Mexico? You can't!" Julia held up her index finger. "First, you can't leave the county." Then, another finger joined the first and she stabbed them in his direction as she spoke. "Second, you have to go back in with me and tell them I didn't bail you out."

"Julia, think it through. I can't tell them who did, so why would they believe me if I told them you didn't?"

"I don't know. But we have to try."

"I can't."

"What?"

"Look, as soon as I find out who's behind all this, I'll get word to you."

"You can't do this to me."

He grasped both of her shoulders, and the touch sent a jolt through him like a runaway bull in Pamplona. He struggled to force it down. "I'm sorry," he told her.

Julia's brow furrowed with hurt that he wanted to wipe away. Instinct overrode common sense, and he tried to ease the pain from her eyes with a gentle caress across the freckles on her cheek.

She didn't pull away. Then, the lines around her mouth relaxed as he ran a finger lightly over her lips. She parted them, and it was his undoing. He lowered his head and kissed her.

Gently.

Slowly.

He savored the taste of her.

She began to move with him, to match his kiss and deepen it. The long months of celibacy took hold of him. He pulled her into his embrace as his tongue drifted over her lips, parting them.

He was on fire.

And if the grip she had on his shirt was any indication, so was she.

Maria!

His knee moved between her legs and only then did he realize she was shaking. He moved his head back to see her and was surprised at the deep auburn hair. It should be black. Why wasn't it the shining black he knew so well?

Grief froze his ardor, if not his lust. This was not Maria. Hawk backed away, leaving Julia only the car for support. He couldn't do this. It would never be fair to either of them. "I am so very sorry."

"For what? The kiss?" Julia sucked her lips in as if blotting lipstick. "Or for deserting me in the midst of this nightmare?"

He squirmed. "I want to help you."

"Then stay and help me find out what's going on."

"I can't." He grasped her shoulders, ignoring the currents that ran up his arms. "I promise you, I will return. I will find out who has done this to you. And I will make sure he pays."

With one last look of regret, he turned and jogged away. Within moments, he was gone from sight.

Julia stared after Hawk, a hand pressed against lips still burning from his kiss. She'd gone from furious to sex-starved with one touch of his hand. She was still flaming with desire. She wanted to finish what they'd started, to put out the fire, even as her anger mounted.

He'd deserted her. And right now, that bothered her more personally than professionally, which pissed her off even more.

She got into her car and drove back to the office to think. She'd find a solution, with or without the pirate's help. She just needed time to sort it all out.

Hakon Thoralssen I stormed past his secretary's desk and, in an atypical show of emotion, slammed his office door. It didn't latch and, in fact, came ajar just enough so that his voice carried to the foyer.

A conscientious assistant would have gotten up and quietly closed the door. Kate Milden chose to utilize the rare advantage. She heard him pound out a phone number, then bark at the person on the other end of the line without ever identifying himself.

"Would you like to explain to me how in the hell my son managed to get out of jail?"

There was a pause.

"That attorney of his knows breach of ethics. She would never bail him out. You know damn well that's why she was chosen. And if she didn't, someone else did. Someone we're not aware of. Find out who it is."

A longer pause.

"I don't care. Find out. The man is a monumental danger to our plans. He must be stopped."

Silence for a moment, except for some rustling papers.

"No. You find out who posted bail. I have a pretty good idea where he's run to and it's time to accelerate my plans. I'll take care of my son. And that village of his."

The sound of the phone hitting the cradle with some force was the last thing Kate heard. She raced to the foyer entry with a file and posed as if just returning when the inner door abruptly opened. Mr. Thoralssen glared at her with accusation filled eyes.

"Where have you been?"

"I'm sorry, Mr. Thoralssen. I went to the file room for an additional record. Is there something you need?"

He stared at her for a long moment, and she met his stare calmly.

"No. Nothing at all. Call my car. I have an errand to run." He went back into his office, closing the door firmly behind him.

After the car had been called and the very tense owner of Thoralssen Industries left, Kate went into his office to place a file on his desk and noticed a folder she did not recognize. Lifting up a corner, she saw a photograph of what appeared to be an exotic locale, a beautiful little bay that overlooked a white sand beach. The top half of the picture had been torn off, so she had no way of determining where the picture was from.

Kate returned to her desk and tore a page of notes out of her steno pad. Crumbling it up as if to toss in the trash, she instead inserted it into her bag beside the wastebasket.

Right next to the paperwork labeled Sure Deal Bail Bonds.

The drive to her office had yielded no workable ideas for Julia. She sat at her desk and stared at the legal pad in front of her. This always facilitated brainstorming, but any help deserted her this afternoon. She did not have a single clue how to proceed.

Once again, her intercom buzzed at the same instant Paul Benton stormed in.

"Mr. Benton," came through in the voice Gail reserved for people she considered lowlifes.

Damn.

"Paul," Julia said, plastering on a smile. "What a surprise."

"I doubt that. You know exactly why I'm here." He plopped down into a chair.

"Please. Enlighten me."

"You bailed your own client out of jail?"

Double damn.

"No. Actually, I didn't." Julia willed her smile to stay in place.

"That's not what the records say."

"I am aware of what they say."

"Well? If you didn't, who did?"

Julia set her pen down on the desk with a practiced ease. "I have absolutely no idea."

"I find that a little hard to believe."

As much as she preferred to kick Mr. Paul Benton right into the nether worlds, Julia got up and walked to the window instead, praying the distance would help.

It didn't. In no time, Paul Benton was beside her, placing his sleazy hand on her shoulder. Mr. Smooth was back. "I don't know how long I can keep the partners from learning about this."

Julia turned away and went to the sideboard to pour a glass of water, trying to affect a casual attitude. But her hands shook so badly, she thought she might drop the pitcher. She set it down without pouring.

"What are you here to tell me, Paul?"

"Right to the point as always, eh, Julia? That's one of many things I like about you. Okay. You want it between the eyes. I'll give it to you. You've got forty-eight hours to determine who bailed out your client. I'll protect you that long. After that, there's no way I can keep the partners from finding out."

"I understand."

"You'd better. Your professional integrity isn't the only thing on the line here. Your entire career is at stake. I know just how important that is to you."

"Yes," she ground out.

"Then get me the information I need."

After Paul Benton left her office, Julia sat down at her computer and looked up Tierra Bonita del Dios. Then, she picked up the phone. An hour later, she stopped in front of her assistant's desk.

"Clear my calendar, Gail."

"What's up, boss?"

"I'm going to Mexico."

CHAPTER FIVE

"Tierra Bonita de Dios," Julia muttered. Hawk's village in Mexico was named Beautiful Land of God. After two days of travel, the sun-bleached landscape seemed more like the Devil's corridor than a God-given land.

She hadn't listened to her premonitions and now here she sat, hot, thirsty, and roaring down a dirt road in a school bus well past its prime.

Necessity forced her to share what felt like a single seat with an obese woman and small child. Both, according to Julia's nose, were in need of a bath. She watched as the little girl wiped her runny nose for the umpteenth time, then wiped her hand on the side of a faded summer dress. Julia tried to squirm, but legs clammy with sweat seemed permanently glued to the ripped vinyl seat. Shorts had made sense in the heat. Now, she wasn't so sure.

That king-sized cretin, Hawk, was going to pay for this if she ever found him.

Correction. When she found him. No grubby, antiquated bus was going to throw her off the scent.

"Oof!" Julia went airborne again, leaving at least one layer of skin on the seat, as the tired, old bus catapulted over yet another rut in the road. One hand had a death grip on the seat in front of her. The other clenched a rapidly aging guidebook.

She was the only gringo aboard a bus filled to overflowing with villagers and an equal number of chickens, pigs, and various other animals. And the only one with decent hearing, if the blaring salsa music was any indication.

She should have known better. The first forewarning had come in San Diego when she couldn't get a flight out that day to the closest large city. Mexico City had been her only option. She'd ignored the warning and rushed off to the airport, picking up one of those standard issue guide books.

Warning number two. She had three hundred and fifty miles to travel once her plane landed. She should never have disembarked. Unable to get a bus out until the next morning, she'd checked into the local hotel and was soon dead to the world in air-conditioned comfort.

Sleeping through her alarm should have been her third warning. Once again, instead of listening, she'd made a mad dash for the only bus of the day to Oaxaca just as the morning sun crested the Sierra Madres. Lulled by smooth roads and cushy seats, she dozed through most of the trip, catching only fleeting glances of lush, mountainous landscape and occasional dots of habitation that must be villages.

Oaxaca was a verdant, bustling city nestled in the valley between two mountain ranges. It was also where her pleasant, pampered world came crashing to an end. With fifty miles to go, only one mode of transportation presented itself—the chicken buses.

So now, three hours later, sitting on an overfull bus and still not used to the pungent stench of pig, Julia prayed for an end. How much further could it possibly be? And what would she have to ride next? A burro?

Stifling another urge to gag, Julia fanned herself with the guidebook and longed for her air-conditioned condo. She could be sunk deep into the soft-stuffed leather couch, feet up, sipping a cool drink.

Heaven.

The bus bounced over another pothole and her teeth rattled right along with it. Of course, anything would feel like heaven compared to this.

That swamp rat! She could hardly wait to get her hands on Mr. Hakon Thoralssen II. A comic strip vision came to mind. Julia, a.k.a. The Compeller, a smartly-dressed heroine who fights injustice the world over, stands boldly in front of her towering foe, Hawkman. She advances slowly. He backs up, fear evident in his eyes. Just then…

Plop! Julia looked at the gray glop of goo oozing down her T-shirt, then up at the caged birds on the rack above her.

"Ugh." *Oh, yes. The bastard will pay. I don't care how big he is. Somehow, he will pay.*

Just then, the bus skidded to a halt, and Julia's knees struck the seat in front of her.

"Tierra Bonita!" the driver yelled.

"Thank God!" Julia jumped up and hit the rack above her seat, setting the birds to squawking.

"Espera!" she cried, holding her aching head. "Espera, por favor. Wait! This is my stop." She climbed over her seatmates and wove her way through the tangle of bodies to the front of the bus.

Julia froze as she got her first look out the front window. This was not good. No town surrounded them. In fact, there wasn't a building or piece of civilization anywhere she could see. Only scrawny trees, brush and road. Dredging up more of her high school Spanish, she turned to the driver.

"Este es Tierra Bonita?"

"Si, si." He waved for her to move.

She clutched her lone suitcase and stepped off the bus, turning back to the driver and almost getting bowled over by two men as they exited.

Thud!

Julia jumped when several baskets and boxes hit the ground next to her. She turned back to the driver as the doors screeched shut.

"Wait! Espera! Donde esta la...cuidad?" She yelled. Was that the right word for village?

All she got was another backhanded wave as the bus started out. Julia stared as her only lifeline roared away, leaving nothing but the rank smell of diesel and dust in its wake.

Coughing, she turned to the men, but they'd disappeared, boxes, baskets and all. She did a complete circle.

Nothing.

There was no telling when another bus would be by. She'd asked for a schedule in Oaxaca, but the man just laughed. She gathered the bus runs were sporadic at best.

Sweat trickled a path along her spine as the sun beat down and panic edged its way inside her mind.

"Take a deep breath, girl," she told herself. *In through the nose. Out through the mouth. Slow it down. Relax.*

What a fool's journey this had become, chasing after a pirate, of all things. What was she thinking? Her eyes narrowed. If the man had stayed in San Diego like he should have, she wouldn't be in this fix. An image of Hawk splayed out in the sand, captive to the baking sun, brought a grimly satisfied smile to her face.

Julia reached for her half-empty bottle of water and took a comforting swallow as she surveyed the landscape more closely. Those men had gone somewhere.

Then, she saw it. A small, barely visible path through the brush.

With no other option available, she picked up her bag and headed down the footpath. It was flat and dry at first and she made good time. Green became the predominant color as the landscape transformed itself from arid brush to tropical forest.

"Ka-kaw!"

Julia jumped, and her eyes darted from side to side as she tried to identify the noise. When she saw the colorful bird on a nearby tree branch, she sagged onto a fallen log in relief.

Wiping more sweat from her forehead, she took another sip of her water and checked the bottle. There wasn't much left. Only a couple more swallows. She must be on the right path. It was the only one. Julia mouthed a silent prayer that she wasn't on a wild goose chase.

A skittering noise beside her was all she needed to go flying off the log, hands outstretched to ward off a blow. A small lizard crawled onto the wood and stared curiously up at her.

She took long, deep breaths to still her frantic heart. Walking again, Julia glanced back every so often to make sure the critter didn't follow her.

This trail led somewhere.

Didn't it?

After what seemed like hours, the path began to switchback and slope steeply downhill. It also narrowed as vines and other greenery crowded the path. The air was laden with an oppressive heat and she had trouble drawing a satisfying breath.

Soon the vines thickened enough to slice at her legs. She took exaggerated steps in an effort to evade them. When that didn't work, she used her jacket-covered arm to bushwhack them out of her way. With each swing, she designated a new name for her nemesis.

Moron.

Swing.

Sewer scum.

Swing.

Worthless pile of shit.

She stopped to wipe sweat off her face. Her feet felt like they were on fire from the ground heat seeping through her thin sandals. She'd finished the last few drops of her water hours ago.

Swing.

Chowder head.

Swing.

Fleabag.

Julia stopped to rest. Her throat was as dry as a sheet in a dust storm. With her water gone, she struggled to work up some spit. Nothing. She tried to swallow, but her throat squeezed shut. And stuck, like the vines that kept attacking her feet.

Tighter. And tighter.

Oh, shit.

She gasped, desperate for air.

Shit. Shit. Shit.

Her heart was running a marathon, pulling her along with it. The trees moved. No. It wasn't the trees. It was her. Branches scraped at her legs as she fell with a thunk to the ground.

She tried again to clear the lump. The tightness eased and Julia gasped, drinking in great gulps of air. She lay for long moments as her heart crossed the finish line and began to settle down.

I'm a complete idiot!

This back country trek was way out of her comfort zone. Hell, up until now, hiking meant lacing up the tennies for a sunny walk along the asphalt Embarcadero on San Diego's waterfront. You always knew where you were, and water was just a tourist shop away.

Julia sat up and looked around. How much further could it be? How long could one survive without water? It seemed like those *Survivor* contestants on TV went a few days before they had drinking water. So she probably wouldn't die from lack of it, today anyhow.

Julia looked up through the canopy of trees. Dusk coated the sky with charcoal and the stark realization hit home that she was going to be stuck out here for the night.

A lone tear escaped and wandered slowly down her cheek. She caught the salty droplet with her tongue, then shook her head and stood up. Damn it! This forest was not going to win. That would mean Hawk had won, and that would not happen.

Ripping the vines away from her legs, she went back to work, slashing her way through.

It took another hour of whacking away, with an equal amount of time spent resting, before the vines gave way to a path of dried mud. The shrubbery began to disappear as a wall of dirt and hard mud rose up in front of her. This must be the mud flow that had destroyed the village.

Julia bent over, hands on her knees, and waited for her labored breathing to slow. Finally. She must be close.

A barely passable trail had been carved out of the mud, so she eased into the opening. It felt—closed in, with a mud wall on either side that was taller than her head. A cave junkie could get claustrophobic in here.

Mindful of the dirt-caked walls, she didn't see the path widen in front of her as she cleared the mountain of mud. She didn't see the distance to the ground beyond it, either. Her foot set down on nothing but air and she screamed as she did a freefall plunge out of the mud.

An obstacle broke her fall. Not an obstacle exactly. Arms. Big, tanned, gorilla arms. She followed them up to massive shoulders she'd seen before, attached to a neck with corded veins pumping away, either from exertion or irritation. Her head raised higher still and she gazed into the scowling face of Hakon Thoralssen II.

All the names she designed during her trek vanished as she swayed. "Savior," she croaked, then darkness became her only reality.

What the hell was the woman thinking? If he'd had any idea she would try to follow him, he'd...well, he didn't know what he'd have done. He never considered the possibility that she would be this driven.

Damn it! He did not have time to nursemaid some city-slicker who no doubt would exhaust every last bit of her energy trying to drag him back to San Diego.

Julia began thrashing in bed, and he closed the distance between them. He reached for her arms and pinned them to her side with his body, running his hands along her hair and down the side of her face. It had proven to be the only thing that calmed the demons in her dreams.

"No!" She screamed the words. Then, in a much weaker voice, she whispered. "Help me, Hawk. Help me."

"Shhh. Shhh. I'm here. You're safe." He kept saying the same words over and over, until she stilled and he could release her. He felt her hot forehead for the umpteenth time. Her fever still raged. The bowl of water had turned tepid. Rather than leave her to get cooler water, he swished the rag around in what he had. He wrung it out and placed it across her forehead.

Hawk stood and ran shaking fingers through his hair. He'd never known anyone to go to these lengths to prove a point. There was much more to Julia Branholt than he'd first imagined. And he'd imagined much more than he should have.

While she slept, Hawk packed up a few of his things. He glanced at her over his shoulder. She would not be here long. He'd make sure of that. But while she was here, he could bunk over at Manuel and Mama Rosa's hut.

The door opened and Claire Gaetani poked her head in. "Want me to spell you?"

"No. I'll stay with her." Holding up the bowl, Hawk asked if she would get him fresh water.

After what seemed like hours, Hawk stood to stretch shoulders too long hunched over before placing yet another cool rag across Julia's forehead. Her face seemed less flushed. He felt her cheek. She was cooler.

The fever had broken.

Thank God. Hawk put his hands over his face and let his relief and gratitude wash over him.

Julia would be all right.

Rubbing eyes too long open, he went to get Claire. He could sleep now.

A faint smell found its way into Julia's consciousness. She turned into the pillow, inhaling a scent like wood smoke, layered with something tangy, like salt. A lighter floral scent topped the mixture.

She slid a tongue that seemed doubled in size across the back of her teeth. Heavy eyelids resisted her attempts to open them, so Julia took it slow and easy until she could see her surroundings better.

She was in a room, of sorts. More like a hut of sticks or reeds twined together. The roof was a dark, dense, dirty-looking thatch. Still, the open-air windows in every wall let in enough light to dispel the gloom. Wild orchids wound their way in through the nearest window and climbed the walls. Julia smiled at this bit of beauty in the midst of rustic basics.

She eased herself up and her hazy world warped into a moving carnival mirror. Sour nausea crawled up from her stomach, and she leaned her head toward her shoulder in an attempt to stop the spinning.

The door opened and a woman entered who looked familiar in a wavy, mirage kind of way. Julia squinted in the hope it would help to dispel the dizzies. It didn't work.

She must have swayed because the woman put a hand on her shoulder, steadying her. "Take it easy, Julia. Don't get up too quickly."

"Who—" Her tongue still felt uncooperative. She tried again. "Where am I?"

The woman smiled. "You're in Tierra Bonita."

"Hawk's village. I made it, then." She could see the far end of the room she was in now. A simple desk and chair were set against a wall filled with drawings and maps.

"Yes. But I don't know how." The woman filled a glass with a tangerine-colored liquid and held it out.

"It was stupid." Julia reached for the glass and got it on the first try.

"Still dizzy?"

"Not so much now."

"Nausea?"

"Fleeting." She took a sip of the cooling juice.

"Headache?"

"Oh, yes."

"That will ease. You had a touch of sun stroke, and we were pretty worried."

"How long have I been out?"

"You landed in Hawk's arms"—the woman paused—"last evening. It's mid-morning now."

Julia blushed at the flash of strong arms and ice-blue eyes.

"Ah. No problems with your memory, then."

Julia took a good at the woman. The long, frosted hair, heart shaped face, and brown eyes seemed familiar. "I know you. You visited Hawk in jail, right? With your husband, Dion Gaetani?"

"Yes. I'm Claire."

"The agent who arrested my client," Julia said stiffly.

"The client who has you on this ill-equipped bounty hunt," Claire shot back.

Ready to retort, Julia stopped and began to chuckle. "Touché."

Claire laughed, too, and took a seat beside her on the bed. "I cannot believe you found your way cross-country to this village."

"Me neither."

"Even I didn't try that trick. You know, it took a lot of work by hand to carve a path through that mudslide. It only got opened a couple of weeks ago. Before then, the only way to access the village was by boat."

Julia nodded as she set her juice down.

"So," Claire continued, "why didn't you just come by boat?"

Julia stared at Claire, speechless. Then, she flopped back onto the bed, laughter bubbling out of her even as she clutched her pounding head. "I—never even thought about it," she managed to gulp out.

Hawk paused just inside the door and observed them as they laughed. He hadn't really listened to that sound in a long time. Too long. It reminded him of better times. He reached for the door frame, fighting for breath, until the wave of sorrow passed. Normally, he could suppress the memories. Somehow, though, every time he was around his attorney, they blindsided him.

He remembered everything from last night. The softness of her hair, the curves he tried not to see as he changed her into clean clothes found in her bag. Hell, even the way she said his name echoed over and over in his mind. Julia's arrival here had gutted him in a way he did not want to acknowledge.

Julia Branholt was a complication he didn't need. What he needed was time to investigate who was bent on sabotage of the village recovery efforts. Hawk frowned. So why, watching Claire and Julia now, did he sense the irritating sentiment that some load had been lifted from his shoulders?

"Something funny?" he said, a little too sharply.

The laughter died, and Hawk found he missed it.

Both women sat up and Claire reached out to steady a still shaky Julia.

"Be careful. You've been down and out for several hours," Claire said. "Don't try to do too much, okay?"

Julia nodded, keeping her dark blue eyes focused on Hawk's face. Eyes that, when matched with the thin line of her lips, appeared to have a few things to say. Odds weren't in his favor that they were complimentary, either.

Claire put the cup of juice back in Julia's hand, wrapping her fingers snugly around it. "Drink."

Again, Julia nodded.

On her way out the door, Claire paused next to Hawk, glancing back at Julia. "I thought you were going to get some sleep. You were up all night."

"I had things to tend to."

She tapped his arm. "Be nice. I know you are very aware just how rough a time she's had."

He glared at her.

She smiled sweetly, but didn't back off. "And don't let her overdo it, either. She still has a headache and could relapse."

"All right. I get it. Go easy on the woman."

Impulsively, he kissed her cheek. Claire was a caring woman and would make a great mom. Hawk smiled. Dion was a lucky man.

After Claire left, he turned back to the problem at hand. Her wide open eyes in such a pale face gave her the appearance of ghost.

She'd damn near become one.

Every protective instinct in him clawed its way to the surface like a drowning man screaming for air and he clenched his fists behind his back. He needed to hit something. Instead, he lashed out at the only thing he could. "What in the hell were you thinking?"

Julia's eyes narrowed. "I was thinking about getting your ass back to San Diego to get me out of the hot seat."

"Damn it! This isn't some urban park with groomed trails and water stations every two miles. This is the tropics and it can be as dangerous as the Australian outback." He pulled her up from the bed then, fighting an intense urge to crush her to him. "My God, Julia. You could easily have died out there."

"Yes, well, I didn't." She swayed.

"Whoa, there." Shit. Remorse squeezed the air out of his lungs. He was an idiot for baiting her in this condition. Hawk pulled her against him and let her use him for support. She seemed so frail as her arms snaked around him and she laid her head on his chest.

He forced himself to breathe in and out in measured tones while she rested. Inside, the stirring of long-repressed desire exploded like a starved lion prepared to pounce on his prey. He went rock hard in an instant.

Julia shuddered, and Hawk dug deep to squelch his hunger, helping her to sit down on the bed. He gripped the edges of the crude wooden dresser as the weight of remorse settled on his shoulders and iced his libido. He would not betray Maria.

He handed her juice to her, and backed up until he could lean against the wall. "You all right?" His concern came out sounding more like an inconvenienced ogre than someone who actually cared.

"Sure." Julia glared at him. "I'm just ducky. Why wouldn't I be?" She gulped some juice, then took another, slower sip. "This juice is outstanding, yet I can't place the taste."

"It's a guava-mango combination, along with a few other local fruits," Hawk answered, stuffing his hands in the pockets of his khaki shorts. "It helps to counteract the heat and, in your case, replenish dehydration."

"Dehydration I wouldn't have if..." Her voice trailed off as she rubbed her temple. "What did Claire mean, that you'd been up all night?"

Hawk's mouth tightened. *Thanks, Claire.* "Nothing."

"Oh." Julia watched him for a moment, and then stood. Hawk reached for her elbow, but she brushed him away. "Coming here was a stupid thing to do," she said with a sigh.

"Yes. It was."

Hawk saw the not-so-subtle change in her eyes. Even with translucent shadows underneath, they could still hurl ice missiles like an Olympic javelin thrower.

"If you hadn't jumped bail, I wouldn't be traipsing all over the *outback* to find you."

"And if you weren't such a control freak, you'd have recognized I'd come back as soon as I resolved issues here."

"Just how would I know that?"

Hawk moved in front of her. He reached out to shift a piece of auburn hair that had fallen across her cheek. Soft. Just as he'd remembered. His hand lingered. "You know more about me than anyone else outside of this village, counselor. Do you really think I'd have left you with that mess if there'd been any other choice?"

She didn't move from his touch, but placed a hand on the closest piece of furniture. "No."

"Then trust me now. Go home and let me finish here. I'll come back as soon as I can."

"I can't."

He arched his eyebrows. "Can't?"

Angry eyes flashed. "Okay. I won't. If I go back without you, I might as well hand my career over to the law review."

He lowered his hand. "It's an easily explained misunderstanding. You simply need to find out who really posted bail."

"It's not that simple."

"Why not?"

Julia didn't answer him, which meant he'd touched a sore spot she wasn't ready to talk about. Hawk wondered if she ever confided in anyone.

She touched one of the orchids intertwined with the reeds that made up the walls of his room. "These are beautiful."

He waited for a moment, wondering if he should push the issue. The added worry seemed to deepen the dark circles under her eyes. He wanted to wipe them away.

But he couldn't. He had commitments of his own.

"Would you like to see more?" he finally asked, wondering why he'd made the offer. He should be tossing her on a California-bound boat. Instead, he'd chosen to play tour guide?

The deep lines of worry etched in her face eased as she considered his request. "Yes," she said. "I think that would be nice."

He closed his eyes, mentally shoved his misgivings to the back of his mind and buried his qualms even deeper. "Well then, counselor," he said, holding out his arm, "let me show you why this village is named God's Beautiful Land."

CHAPTER SIX

Julia would have preferred a smile. An arm to lean on certainly seemed a conciliatory offer, but that boyish grin was absent. Somewhere, deep inside, a tendril of regret wound its way to her heart and lungs, generating a sigh that escaped unfettered.

"Are you all right?" he asked as they left the small, one-room house.

"Fine." *Except that, against all reason, I would give anything for you to turn that dazzling smile my way.*

"No dizziness?"

Only when you're near. "Not anymore," Julia answered.

"Then let me show you my home."

Hawk took it easy on her. They walked through the village as if it was a Sunday afternoon stroll. He kept it light, showing her the new single unit structures they were building for the families. All the materials were local, some even coming from the ruins left after the mudslide.

"The village elders feel using these materials is a tribute to those who did not survive. A way of remembering." His voice dropped to a murmur. "As if we could forget."

He stared off into the distance for a long moment and Julia wanted more than anything to wipe the shadows away. She raised her hand, but hesitated when his face twisted into that of a lion engaged in the fury of attack. Hawk kicked at the pile of wood on the ground, sending it flying. His sandaled feet must have stung from the movement, but he didn't show it. Instead, he shook his head, and then bent over to right the wood pile.

By the time he finished, the façade of contentment was firmly back in place and their tour continued. Hawk showed Julia how they'd managed to modernize the homes, pumping water up from the community cistern with a windmill driven pump. Yet they still used the local stucco and wood building methods. The roofs were still thatch, and no home had more than two rooms.

"We decided, as a village, to maintain the indigenous traditions with the new structures."

Julia glanced at the row of single occupant buildings. "Ah, then that's the reason for the outhouses."

The lines around his eyes crinkled the tiniest little bit. "Funny. No, it would be nice to have indoor plumbing. However, we first need to find a way to put septic systems in." He shrugged. "It's on the list. After we are done with the reconstruction." Hawk frowned. "We can't even proceed with that until we locate more funding, though."

"Legally, this time, if at all possible, okay?" Julia said.

Amazed, she watched the color rise in his face. He scratched the back of his neck as he answered. "If I'd had any other option, I would have taken it."

"I'm not so sure," she said. "You seem to enjoy the life of a rogue."

Wrinkles returned to his face for entirely different reasons, dousing the momentary spark in his blue eyes. "I didn't always."

Julia immediately regretted the dig. "I know."

Hawk showed her some of the furniture that Claire had built. The style was basic and utilitarian, but with each one created specifically for the owner. This headboard had the design of a whale for little Tomas. That chair had extra padding for Mama Rosa, who complained about her rheumatism.

"She's quite talented, isn't she?" Julia asked, admiring a dresser inlaid with tiny pieces of shell.

Hawk smiled. "Yes. We're very lucky to have her."

A tiny green string pulled at Julia's heart.

Next, Hawk showed her the devastation up close. A crew of ten or so men were busy shoveling mud and debris into rough-hewn wheelbarrows.

"We work hard and slowly reclaim our land. When full, the wheelbarrows are taken down near the beach and sorted into use or discard piles. Then the remaining mud and rock is thrown in the water on the far side of the breakfront. The village unanimously decided to do that in the hopes that it would fortify the rocky shoals and help protect Tierra Bonita as the winter storms roll in."

"You think of everything, don't you?"

"No." He swept his hand around. "They do."

An older man pushed a wheelbarrow piled high with mud and debris, his arms straining with the effort. He stopped when he reached the two of them. Upon closer inspection, the man was difficult to categorize. His hair, coal black with little or no gray, said he was young. Yet the lines in his face said he had seen much of life.

Now, with his dark brown eyes on her, Julia felt he saw through her with a wisdom born from ages of living. Was he some sort of shaman or village elder? It was almost as if he peeled away the outer layers of her skin and found her spiritual core, both good and bad, all mixed together.

Julia crossed her arms over her chest to dispel the sensation that she'd just gone through some sort of test. And been found wanting. The man still did not smile.

"Hola, Manuel. Como esta?" Hawk said.

"The mud continues to fight us, but we will win," the man answered in broken English, slapping Hawk on the back.

Julia expelled the air she'd been holding in.

"I have no doubt." Hawk grinned. "Julia, this is Manuel. You will most likely meet his wife, Rosa, at tonight's meal. Together, they pretty much run the village, and rightly so." He nodded at Manuel. "The man has more sense in his big toe than most people have in their entire body."

Manuel shook his head at the praise, but his wide grin showed his pleasure. He lapsed into his native Spanish. "Por lo tanto, que muestran la hermosa señorita nuestro pueble, ¿eh?"

"Si, si," Hawk answered. "I am showing Julia around."

"Te ves bien juntos."

Hawk began to fidget and Julia wondered what they were talking about. She'd heard the words. Hermosa señorita. Pretty woman. Were they discussing her? Maybe she had passed the test.

"Usted sabe que no es asi," Hawk said.

"Que deberia ser. Usted ha sido demasiado tiempo solos, mi hijo. Usted necesita una mujer a su lado."

Mujer meant woman. They were definitely talking about her. Julia watched Hawk. He seemed almost angry at the man. His next words, whatever they were, came out harshly.

"Nadie nunca sustituir a ella."

He stalked off without another word, leaving Julia staring at his back. She turned to ask Manuel, but he hefted the wheelbarrow to move on. The grin on his face, coupled with the wink he tossed at her, answered her question. She nodded toward him. She most definitely had passed.

As she followed after Hawk, Julia's smile disappeared. What had Manuel said to upset him? And what did it have to do with her? She walked past the last of the mud and debris and paused in amazement at the idyllic little cove in front of her.

The tranquil blue-green water outdid any travel brochure she'd ever seen. Lazy waves tapped a white sand beach unmarred by rock or driftwood. On one side, a pier jutted out toward a rocky promontory that, according to Hawk, held the occasional ferocity of the ocean at bay. On the other, the beach disappeared around a corner. Beyond the entrance to the cove the Pacific Ocean seemed to go on to infinity.

Adding to the ambiance, an old wooden schooner rested at anchor in the harbor. Dion and Claire's boat, Julia surmised. *The Treasure.*

Hawk stood near the shore, stiff and unmoving.

Her lack of energy caught up to her, and Julia sat down to wait, running handfuls of the fine sand through her fingers. Whatever Manuel had told Hawk brought back the deep lines of pain to his face. With shoulders drooped and hands buried in his pockets, he watched the water silently.

The realization that he was thinking about Maria hit her right in the heart, and she threw the sand away in disgust. She wanted to bring back his smile. When had she come to care about a beach bum turned pirate who lived in backwoods Mexico?

Julia pulled her knees up and laid her head on them. There were so many reasons why she should never fall for Hawk. She had a life in the city. Well, maybe not a life, exactly. But her job was important to her. She was good at it and she did good things through it. Not to mention the fulfillment of that long held promise to her father. She would succeed. Nothing must get in the way of that. Nothing. Julia doubted Hawk would understand that.

Even if he could get past his longing for Maria, she couldn't see him living for any length of time in San Diego. She glanced around. Pretty or not, this place would drive her nuts before long.

No, there was no room for Hakon Thoralssen II in her life. She needed to keep this relationship strictly business.

Julia stood and, realizing she didn't know the way back to where she slept, walked over to Hawk's side.

"Can you swim?"

She jumped as he spoke. "What?"

"Can you swim?"

"Um, yes."

"We'll swim out to the schooner. You can spend the afternoon with Claire, and I'll collect you later for dinner."

His voice was almost normal and all business. The loss of the companionship they'd shared left a hole in her heart.

"I'm pretty tired."

"I'll help you if necessary."

She followed him into the water and he set a leisurely pace for the schooner. It wasn't far, but she soon felt the strain and her strokes slowed. Hawk stayed at her side the whole time. When they reached the boat, he climbed aboard first, and then bent down to help her up the ladder. The sense of protection that these small actions evoked threatened to overwhelm her. She knew he would not let harm come to her. Underneath, a much more basic feeling wound its way through her body. She wanted to be caressed with the same gentle caring he showed her now. She wanted him to put a stop to the burn that smoldered deep inside her.

Julia felt her feet touch solid ground as he set her on deck and lamented the loss of his touch when he released her.

"Ahoy, the *Treasure*," he called out as they boarded.

Claire turned with a smile from the chore of taking laundry off the line. "Welcome aboard!"

"Can Julia stay here with you for a while?"

"Certainly."

"I don't want to be an imposition," Julia said.

"Trust me," Claire laughed and plopped into a deck chair. "I'm grateful for the respite. I hate laundry!" She turned to Hawk. "Did Dion catch up with you?"

"I haven't seen him since this morning."

"He has some news."

"I'll find him." He didn't look at Julia, just tossed a hasty "I'll be back later," stepped onto the railing and dove cleanly into the water, swimming back to shore with long, sure strokes.

Oh, yes, he definitely took it easy on me.

The evening sun blanketed the land with a last golden gift. Julia recognized a harmony between man and nature most people rarely glimpsed. She leaned back against the mast, unsure if it was the gentle see-saw of the schooner that relaxed her or the sweet cactus wine. Muscles that spent years bound tighter than a geisha's feet were slowly releasing their hold. She smoothed the fabric of the tropical sun dress Claire had loaned her. Maybe wearing something so different from her wardrobe of dark suits was why she felt so calm and content.

She followed the waning sun lines as they highlighted the village. New huts gleamed with fresh paint, still surrounded by the scraps of homes shredded by the mud. There was a lot still to be done here.

"You look pretty content," Claire said as she stepped on deck.

"I am. I don't think I've been this relaxed since...Hawaii."

"Ooh, Hawaii. Dion's promised me a voyage there as soon as he feels comfortable taking a couple of weeks away from here." She placed a hand on her growing belly. "Of course, junior here might cause a bit of a delay. I hear Hawaii is lovely."

"It is. Or at least, it was when I was there. It's been over eight years." Flashes of sultry nights spent making love on the beach and a laid back lifestyle she barely remembered now crossed Julia's mind.

"The look on your face tells me there's a story to be told."

To Julia's relief, Dion's arrival made answering unnecessary. Hawaii was something she worked very hard to repress. She was all grown up now, and these days, there was no time for the beach.

Dion climbed aboard and wrapped his arms around his wife. After a long kiss that had Julia inspecting the deck, he spoke. "You ladies ready for some supper?" He turned to Julia. "I told Hawk I would bring both of you."

"We're famished," Claire answered, grabbing a shawl as Julia slipped into her sandals.

Dion rowed them ashore and they walked along the path to the one large building in the town. Claire explained that this structure currently held their communal meals. Eventually, they hoped to build kitchens onto the homes being constructed.

As they walked, others passed them, smiling and calling greetings.

"Hola, Dion."

"Buenos noches, Clara." The smile on Claire's face validated that she liked the Hispanic variation on her name.

"Bienvenido, Julia."

Julia gave a little wave. "I don't know any of these people," she whispered to Claire. "How do they know me?"

"We don't get many strangers here," Claire said. Her dimples deepened. "Plus, your entrance was, um, memorable."

"Ugh!" Julia groaned.

Julia watched as, arm in arm, Claire and Dion entered the dining hall. Happy noise drifted out through the open doors, along with mouth-watering aromas. Even as the smell of cooking food set her stomach to rumbling, Julia held back. She came from a world of tight lips and guarded secrets. Even in her own family, dinner was a formal affair. You ate. You appreciated the food, but you didn't talk.

People in these parts seemed to speak freely, if the earlier conversation between Hawk and Manuel was any indication.

They enjoyed life with an enthusiasm that was foreign to her. She rubbed her hands on the skirt of her dress and straightened.

Inside this community building, she found herself in an entirely different world. Where the new village homes were muted earth tones due to the materials used to build them, this large room was awash in color. The walls were each painted a different shade, from terra cotta to gold to a rich, cornflower blue. Unfinished murals depicting village life covered half the wall space.

Rows of tables and chairs lent credence to Julia's growing belief that there was no separation in this village. They ate together, worked together, and played together.

Chaos reigned everywhere and Julia stood rooted to her spot trying to find some order to the bedlam. Her rudimentary command of the language failed her completely as numerous conversations of high-spirited Spanish overlapped.

"Oof!" The breath whooshed out of Julia as a child ran into her and she fell against the wall.

"Perdon!" the dark-haired, wide-eyed little girl said with a child's lilting giggle. Julia smiled in response to the sound. As quickly as she came, the child sprinted off, the chase back on as another girl ran after her.

They barely missed a toddling baby, stopping only long enough to tickle the tears away and gain a toothy grin. A teenage girl's job of setting out plates was noticeably slowed by the sideways glances toward the boy who held the stack for her. The wide grin of new love plastered across his face told Julia these two had a future.

"Bella's in lo-ove! Bella's in lo-ove!" the little girls chanted as they ran by.

The teenage girl identified herself as Bella by the crimson flush that tinged her cheeks. The boy only smiled wider.

A swat from the towel of a petite, gray-haired woman sent the little ones rushing off again. As the woman spied Julia, she rushed over, clapping her hands. "Hola, Julia. Bi-envenido a nuestra casa! Welcome." The woman enveloped Julia in a hug, not an easy feat for someone who only reached five foot nothing and never stopped talking.

"Everyone calls me Mama Rosa. You must do the same."

Julia couldn't gauge the woman's age. Her hair color said mature, but the twinkle in her eyes said she would never be old. The welcome in her voice soothed Julia's qualms as she realized that, for the duration of her time here, she would be considered part of the family.

A growing part of her liked that idea. A lot. "I will, Mama Rosa," she said.

"You have met my Manuel, si?" Not waiting for an answer, Mama Rosa waved her towel in the direction of Claire and

Dion. "Now come. You must sit with your friends. It is time to eat and rejoice in all that this day has blessed us with."

Seated next to Claire, Julia scanned the room until she found him. Hawk. It wasn't hard. He was easily the tallest man there. Dressed in his standard khaki shorts, he'd exchanged his tank top for sleeves. The brilliant red birds of paradise that peppered his blue shirt with blasts of color weren't a huge improvement. Still, those shoulders could make anything look like Armani.

Hawk stood unmoving amidst the bedlam, his eyes focused on her. He caressed her face without moving a muscle, then followed the lines of her neck. Eyes filled with hunger wandered along the deep V neckline of her dress. Julia felt the flush creep up her neck and placed a hand across her chest as his gaze returned to her face. The pots and pans clamoring, the voices, even the colors faded for that fragment of eternity. For one time-freezing moment, his face revealed an intense desire.

"Oomph!"

Julia heard the sound even from this distance and used the distraction to draw a deep, world-righting breath. The two little girls had chosen Hawk as their next victim and launched themselves at him. He threw an arm around each with a mock sternness that was contradicted by his hearty laugh. With a youngster under each arm, he maneuvered beside an overstuffed bean bag chair and tossed first one squealing child, then the other, on top of it.

Grinning, he caught Julia's eye and tipped his head in her direction. She acknowledged the nod with her own broad smile.

The girls raced off to find another victim, and Hawk wandered through the crowd toward her. It took him a while, since most everyone stopped him to talk. He spoke the language like a native, and his ease with these people was apparent.

That level of comfort and respect was something Julia had fought her whole life to attain. For him, it seemed effortless. This was a side of Hawk she hadn't seen before. This Hawk, relaxed, laughing, eyes all crinkled around the edges—this Hawk was too easy to like, and that scared the hell out of her. It took all her will to keep from running for the nearest boat out of Tierra Bonita.

As Julia tried in vain to calm breathing that was rapidly escalating, Hawk extricated himself from the crowd and settled into a chair across from her. His personal wall of neutrality seemed, once again, firmly entrenched on his face.

"You fit in like a natural here," she said.

Hawk shrugged. "It's my home."

Any further discussion was forestalled by the arrival of dinner, consisting of warm, home-made tortillas slathered with a rice and bean mixture. It was more fat grams than Julia ate in a month, but she didn't care. The taste was heavenly and unlike anything she'd eaten before. Certainly different from food she'd eaten at the restaurants in San Diego. She closed her eyes and licked her lips to savor that last little taste.

When she opened them, it was to Hawk's eyes focused on her and filled to the brim with dangerous, raw emotion.

Julia took a gulp of juice to cool her flaming cheeks and wondered how she would ever get Hawk back to San Diego with her professional decorum intact.

A rumbling boom sounded in the distance.

Everyone froze.

As she scanned the room, she saw the open mouths and wide eyes of fear. Julia had lived through enough earthquakes to know the look. This did not feel like a quake, but she wasn't immune to the emotion around her as her pounding heart mirrored their apprehension.

Her dinner started to claw its way up to her throat as she remembered. These people had already endured one tragedy too many.

When a chair fell over on the far side of the room, she flinched right along with everyone else.

A subtle vibration hit the building and sent a wall of terror crashing through the town folk. Rabid panic drove them to the doors. Only one man stood in their way.

Hawk.

Julia glanced at the empty seat. When had he moved? He seemed to bar the doors with nothing but his body. The crowd pressed on him even as he tried to calm them.

"Espera!" he roared. "Wait! Seguridad primero! Safety first! Give us a chance to find out what has happened."

A hand clamped down on her shoulder, and she whipped around to Dion, her heart now at marathon speed. He had his arm around his wife and looked from one to the other, mouthing an urgent "stay" before he went to help Hawk.

It took several long minutes to bring order to the room. Women and children fell back to the tables, some weeping softly, some quiet but with eyes shadowed by leftover dread. The men grouped around Manuel and Hawk in frantic discussion.

Dion returned to Claire with the teenage boy Julia remembered from earlier. "Juan will take you two back to the boat."

Claire protested, but Dion held his ground. He kissed her temple, placed a hand on her stomach and uttered an urgent "I need you safe, wife." Then, he was gone. Before long, only women and children remained as the men went to check the village.

"Come on," Julia said as she made to follow Dion.

"No," Claire said. "Let them go."

"What do you mean? We have to find out what's going on."

Claire's hands moved over her rounding stomach. "We will."

"Then let's go." Julia moved toward the door, her instincts screaming to follow Hawk and find out what had happened.

"No," Claire said again.

Julia swiveled, fully prepared to argue. Claire's face was waffling back and forth between furrowed brow worry and a smooth calm. Calm won out. "We need to go to the boat."

Julia tossed her hands in the air and stared at Claire. Remembering Dion's urgent plea, she fought some pretty strong inner demons. The woman's concern for her unborn child, evident by the fact that her hands hadn't left her stomach, turned the tide and Julia capitulated.

"You're right," she said, struggling to maintain an even tone. "Let's get you back to the schooner."

Once on board, Julia began pacing from one end of the schooner to the other. "This is ridiculous. You and the baby are safe now. I should go back to the village."

"We need to give them time."

"I can't stand this waiting!"

"Dion and Hawk will come when they can. I know my husband. He knows I'm worried and will send word as soon as he can. Until then, we wait."

Claire approached worry from a different direction, apparently. She set out deck chairs "for when the men returned."

She prepared drinks and a snack. Julia tried to help her, but couldn't pull herself away from the railing for long. What was happening? Were they safe? Was he?

Julia watched Claire and realized what was missing most from her own life—the complete trust that Claire and Dion had in each other. She knew he would return to her. Could she ever place that much faith in another person? Julia had always carved her own solitary path in the direction she chose, so she doubted it. Still, it would be nice to have that shoulder available. To know that, whether near or separated, he had your best interests always in the front of his mind.

At that moment, the boy, Juan, appeared on shore and shouted something Julia could not interpret. Then, he flew off back into the dark of night.

"It's okay." Claire turned to Julia. "No one has been injured."

Julia noticed Claire's hands shook as she waved to Juan. Her own weren't very steady as she settled them on Claire's shoulders.

"Dion will join us as soon as he can. Just like you said, I'm sure," Julia said.

Over the next hour, any relief fled as Julia alternately followed Claire's direction and chafed at what had begun to feel like a prison on water.

"Arghhh! How can you stand this?"

"It's not easy, trust me," Claire said.

Scant minutes later, two figures emerged from the woods, entered the water and swam to the boat. As they climbed aboard, Julia handed them towels Claire had ready.

Without waiting for them to dry off, Julia pounced. "What's happened?"

The grim line of Hawk's face answered her. "You remember the mud path you walked through to get here?"

"Yes."

"It's gone."

Claire interrupted, handing what looked like double shots of some sort of whiskey to Dion and Hawk and a glass of cactus wine to Julia, who let her curiosity fly.

"What the hell caused that?" she asked.

Dion glanced at Hawk, who shrugged his shoulders.

"Looks to me like the path through the mud was purposely collapsed. It was blown up," Dion answered. "It'll take weeks to dig it back out again."

"No one's been hurt this time, right?" Claire asked.

"This time? There have been other incidents? With people hurt?" Julia asked all three questions back-to-back.

"A broken arm, a few burns. Nothing serious, thankfully," Claire said.

Julia turned to Hawk. "What, exactly, has been going on here?"

Hawk's face was as immovable as handprints in cement. "It's not your concern."

Dion apparently thought otherwise. "There have been four attempts now to slow or halt the reconstruction," he answered.

The digger in Julia forged on. "How?"

"It's. Not. Your. Concern." Hawk glared at Dion as he spoke to Julia.

Julia whirled on Hawk. "How dare you! You're the one who got me into this mess. 'Help me, Julia,' you said. 'I have to get out of jail,' you begged." She jabbed him in the chest with her fingers. "Well, buster, you're out now. And I'm here because of it. So don't try to tell me I'm not involved. I'm involved,"—she slashed an imaginary line across her forehead—"up to here!"

Hawk's face remained set in stone, a narrowing of his eyes the only way to tell he'd heard her.

Dion forestalled any confrontation by answering her.

"As we said, there have been four attempts so far. Twice now our supplies have been rerouted. We found a way around that little issue, though, so they stepped to the next level. The incident just before you both arrived was a fire in our stock of wood. Clearly arson. They left the can of gasoline, probably as a warning."

"And now they've buckled the trail through the mud," Julia finished, sitting down as the adrenaline rush of calling Hawk out fled her body. She felt decidedly ill as she glanced at him and swore she could actually see the storm clouds gathering over his head. Her stomach went from clenched to queasy to downright ill. Maybe she could blame the feeling on the aftermath of her trek through the woods. She glanced at Hawk. No. Not likely.

Dion hit the railing of the *Treasure*. "Damn! I don't even know where to start."

"There's nothing you can do for now," Claire said, wrapping her arms around her husband. "Maybe the light of day will give us ideas. I think we all need a good night's sleep. I know I do." She said her goodbyes and headed below.

The three of them sat looking glumly out at the water. Finally, Hawk stood.

"There's nothing we can do tonight." He glanced at Julia. "I'll take you back."

Julia peeled down to her bikini and left the borrowed sun dress on board. They swam back to shore and sat together on the beach to dry in silence with only a sliver moon watching.

"It's really quite beautiful here."

The only answer she got was a mumbled "yes."

"I can see why you want to preserve it."

Hawk turned to her. "I want to preserve this village because these people are my family."

"You weren't raised here, right?"

He stood then and paced back and forth. "What the hell does that have to do with anything? I accepted this village as my family, and they accepted me as theirs. The one thing in my life that I truly loved belonged to this village. I will not see it destroyed!"

Julia joined him, her hand grazing his arm. He yanked it away, moving several feet from her.

"You need to go home," he said.

"What?" Her eyes widened in astonishment.

"Go home. I can take care of this. I'll protect this village."

"With your life, at this rate!"

"If that's what it takes..."

"So, what? This is a death wish? Is that it? You want to join your beloved Maria?"

As soon as she said the words, the line she'd crossed opened a gaping chasm between them.

Hawk didn't respond. Worse, he wouldn't even look at her. He headed off in the direction of the mud flow, leaving Julia to find her own way through the village to her room.

CHAPTER SEVEN

Julia rose to the enchanting trill of birdsong and the fragrant smell of orchids. She smiled and stretched, easing still sore muscles.

Then memory invaded the peaceful moment. Sleep had been more elusive than usual last night. She didn't need much. In fact, four hours of sleep usually had her ready for whatever the day threw at her. Last night, though, had proven to be an emotional roller coaster. Attacked by both remorse over her imprudent comment and anger at Hawk's inability to accept help, she'd gotten precious little shut-eye.

You would think the man would want all the help he could get. But no, he wants to send me home to cool my jets until he's solved the mystery. Two steps back and one to the right, eh? Not very damn likely!

Out the window, Julia could see the sun barely risen and she groaned. She thought about trying for more sleep, a luxury in her world. Instead, she threw on the same shorts and T-shirt from yesterday and left her room. She needed coffee.

The village was quiet in the aftermath of last night's incident. She entered the main building where the tantalizing aroma of fresh brewed coffee drew her toward the kitchen. A few women were already working. There was no hustle and bustle like at supper. No animated discussions. Julia sensed a resignation. The sabotage last night had done more than destroy a path. It had withered the spirit of the people who lived here. Hopefully only temporarily.

Mama Rosa walked in carrying a basket of eggs. "Ah, Julia. Bienvenido." Even Mama's voice was subdued today.

The other women nodded and murmured greetings, then turned back to their work.

Regret enveloped Julia like a chill wind, and she found herself searching for an idea that would bring back the joy in these women.

"Buenos Dias, Mama Rosa," Julia said. "Is there something I can do to help?"

"Certainly. Come, we will put you to work."

When Hawk entered the kitchen, he'd expected to stoke the fires for the morning meal. Instead, the ovens were going strong and four women were chatting and laughing as they worked—two dark-haired, one gray, and one with cascading reddish-brown hair.

Hawk stopped short. Julia, with splotches of corn flour on her arms, her clothes, even one cheek, focused hard on forming a tortilla. He watched, enchanted, as she tried and failed once, twice, three times before she finally got a passable tortilla formed. She held it up proudly and was greeted with hoots of laughter and much conversation in Spanish.

She saw Hawk then. Eyes sparkling with fun were hard to resist, and he smiled in response. With a gentle touch, he brushed the flour from her cheek, lingering moments longer than necessary. He couldn't help himself. She felt so good, so soft. Yesterday's sun had kissed her skin and allowed her freckles to darken. He found them enticing. Instinctively, he knew she would not agree.

Her blue eyes drew him in like a siren's song. They widened at his drawn out contact, and Hawk forced his world to return to normal. To cover his gaff, he looked down and took great pains to inspect the sad, little tortilla.

"¿De los errores se aprende?" Hawk turned to the village women. Practice makes perfect?

Laughter rolled off their tongues as, one after the other, they began to wipe tears out of their eyes.

"Ella ha practicado"—Mama Rosa paused to catch her breath—"¡diez veces ya!" She grabbed the counter behind her as another paroxysm of laughter threatened to pull her to her knees. "¡Aye, yi, yi!"

Hawk glanced at Julia, wondering how she was handling the ribbing. Wide eyes sparkled, and her grin said it all. "Ten times?" he asked.

"Oh." She shook her finger at Mama Rosa in mock consternation. "You told on me."

"Si, si. I tell so your man knows. He must learn to cook or starve." She spoke to the others then, obviously translating what she had said, because it set them all off again.

"Si, Es bueno Señor Hawk sabe ya cocinar."

Julia's smile died as she saw the look on Hawk's face. She'd heard his name and could guess what had been said. And what Hawk thought. The village had decided they were a couple.

Hawk turned and walked out without another word.

Julia spent the rest of the morning meal trying to figure out how she felt about the exact same thing that tormented him. The thought of being with Hawk, of being his partner, his friend, his woman...

A shiver wound its way through her. She wanted to comb through that blond mane with her fingers. She wanted to run her hands along the lines of that golden body. She wanted to feel him inside her.

The tap on her shoulder startled her, and she almost dropped the load of plates she was about to put away.

"Yoohoo, Julia," a grinning Claire said.

"Ah, sorry. My mind was...elsewhere."

Claire turned and drew Julia's gaze to where Hawk sulked in the corner of the room. "I know exactly where your mind was. And I approve con mucho gusto."

Julia shook her head. "You too? This whole village has us paired up."

"We see what is in your hearts."

"You hear us fighting. That's about all our relationship is good for."

"That's just foreplay."

"Claire!" Heat rose in Julia's cheeks.

Hawk chose that moment to stomp out of the room, glaring at Julia and Claire. It was as if he knew what they'd said. Julia's blush extended to the roots of her hair at the possibility.

"So," Claire said. "Want to help with some furniture repair?"

Julia rotated a shoulder to ease an ache she was sure would be true pain by the next morning. Claire hadn't been kidding about putting her to work. Apparently, she was better at sanding than making tortillas because Claire had shown her what to do and moved away to glue pieces together.

Julia had sanded until she thought her arms would fall off. Stretching the other shoulder, she wondered if that could actually happen.

"Would juice make it feel better?"

The hairs on the back of her neck tingled, down to the teeniest, tiniest ones. The man's voice could charm a prostitute into giving it up for free.

She took the cup, careful to steer clear of his long, powerful fingers as he released it to her.

She took a sip, then tipped the cup in his direction. "Yes. It does help. Thank you."

"Tired?"

"More tired than if I'd spent the day wrangling with a bunch of DA's in court."

Hawk chuckled, and even that small sound heated her blood up another degree or two.

"I've seen you in court. You fight like a tiger."

"I have to. Otherwise, I'll get swallowed up."

"Is that so terrible?" Hawk's eyes held hers.

"Yes."

"Why?"

Julia shifted on the pile of boards she sat on and the boards reacted, toppling over, sending her cup of juice flying. Only Hawk's quick reaction stopped her from tumbling after the wood. He held her until she found her balance, then backed away and stuck his hands in his pockets.

"Thanks. Again. You seem to be in savior mode today." Julia brushed dirt off shorts that were already beyond cleaning.

"You're welcome."

Together, they re-stacked the boards and Julia sat again, careful not to rock the boat this time.

"So? Back to the courtroom. Why is it so important for you to win?"

"Because I like to win. Isn't that enough?"

"No. There's more to it than that."

He was fast becoming a pain in her butt. "It's complicated," Julia said.

Hawk lounged against the wood shed. "Try me."

Julia kicked at a rock on the ground. This wasn't something she wanted to talk about. It also wasn't something she thought Hawk would understand. No one did.

"I made a promise."

"To whom?"

"My father."

"About?"

"Succeeding. He, um, was also an attorney."

Hawk nodded. "He wanted his daughter to follow in his footsteps."

"No." Julia squirmed again, freezing as the boards wobbled. "He wanted his son to."

That raised an eyebrow. "You have a brother?"

"No." She could almost see his brain putting it all together as he took a long moment.

He shook his head. "You never would have measured up to his standards."

"Really? And you are an expert on familial relationships? You, who won't even talk to your father? Or visit him? Or ask him for help?" She stood and grabbed for the spilled juice cup, ready to end this conversation. Hawk's hand on her shoulder stopped her, but she didn't turn around.

"I know because I spent a good part of my life trying to do the same thing—to measure up. Once I figured out I didn't want to be that person, well, you are aware of how things went after that."

Julia stared at the cup in her hands. "Okay. So maybe you do know." She glanced out over the village. "It doesn't change anything, Hawk. I honor my promises."

"Even if you lose yourself in the process?"

She nodded, Hawaii filling her mind for an instant. "Yes. Even if that's the price." After a pause, she turned to him. "Let me ask you a question. Everything you've done for this village, has it just been for the village? Or did you make Maria a promise?"

Tight lips and the stiff set of his shoulders gave Hawk away.

"I see. So, we're not so different, are we? We're both honor bound by promises that will, most likely, change us for the rest of our lives. And not necessarily for the better." She walked off, unwilling to carry the conversation any further.

That evening, at supper, Julia sat with Claire while Hawk chose the corner farthest away from her. He stared at her. She could feel it. Yet every time she chanced a glance, he was deep in conversation with Manuel or one of the other men.

"Julia?"

A quick mental shake pulled Julia back. "Yes?"

"I said," Claire repeated, "do you want to come back to the boat for a glass of wine after supper?"

"I'd love that. Thank you."

Julia tried to forget about Hawk. She tried to carry on a conversation with Dion and Claire. She tried two glasses of wine.

She even tried reminiscing about Mark in Hawaii. Eight years was a long time. Was he married or still playing the beach bum? He'd taught her so much about taking time to relax and enjoy life. She tried to picture him, but the image that invaded her mind had nothing to do with her old surfer boyfriend. Her vision was of a tall, tanned pirate with bulging muscles and long, flowing blond hair.

No matter what she tried, nothing erased the words Hawk had spoken.

"You never would have measured up to his standards. And you'll lose yourself in the process."

He was right. Still, it didn't change a thing. They were destined to follow different paths.

Dion rowed her back to shore, but she declined his offer to escort her to her door. "Thanks, anyway. I can find my own way."

As he rowed back to the schooner, she felt Hawk's presence behind her, like a warm blanket covered in nettles, before she heard him. What he'd said to her earlier, no matter the truth of it, smarted. He was the last person she wanted to see right now.

"I'll walk you home," he said.

His deep, quiet voice eased the sting, and she fell into step beside him.

Just say it. Tell her how you feel. Hawk waited until they were in front of the door to her hut. "I wish…" He shook his head and tried again. "I'm sorry for what I said earlier."

A wistful smile touched Julia's face and he wanted to make it stay.

"No, you're not."

Hawk chuckled. "You're right. What I am sorry for is that I caused you pain."

"Forget it. You didn't tell me anything I didn't already know."

Stop stalling and just say what you came to say. "I wish I were free…"

Julia looked up at him with wide eyes that said she wouldn't let him off the hook. Whether she knew what he wanted to say or not, he would have to say the words.

Why did she have to look like that? All sexy and vulnerable at the same time. How was a man supposed to cope?

"Look," he said with more gravel in his voice than he intended. When she frowned, he reached out to smooth her forehead. "I respect the hell out of you, counselor," he said. His hand stroked the freckles across her cheek, then he gave in to the urge to run his fingers across lips that were devouring his dreams. "I can't get involved with you."

"I know." Her voice was a bare whisper. "We would never work."

"We've got different priorities," he said, bending to breathe in her floral scent. Now it seemed intermingled with salt air and wood smoke.

"We've got different lives," she said, leaning her head back and branding him as her hand settled on his chest.

He watched her lips move as she spoke. "Completely different."

Damn, but she was beautiful. Hawk shook his head. How was a man to resist such temptation? He gave in.

He held her neck with one hand and kissed her.

Just a touch. That's all he would do. He pulled back, saw her closed eyes, her mouth slightly opened, and covered her lips with his again.

She welcomed him. Opened up to him and let him taste the hint of cactus wine. Her arms wound around him and he growled, tightening his hold, deepening the kiss.

She moaned, and he went rock hard. His hands started to move over, under, and around to the underside of her breast.

Damn, but she felt good. He hadn't felt this way since before...

No!

Hawk froze and the change in him burned Julia like a scalded finger. Maria had come between them. She pulled away and opened her door. "I get it. You're still married. Goodnight, Hawk."

CHAPTER EIGHT

Julia needed a break. After another night of very little sleep and a morning of people surrounding her, she knew that if one more person talked to her or asked her a question, she would scream. She wandered away from the center of town and soon found herself on the path to the mudslide. No one worked in this area today so she got the solitude she craved.

She needed time to think. About last night and what she was going to do with these feelings that would not disappear.

Julia reached the flow and moved along its edge until she came to the shattered remnants of the mud pathway.

There wasn't much to see. The trail was intact for about ten feet, then a wall of mud stopped any forward progress. There was no explosive projection of debris, just piled dirt and mud. The blast must have happened on the far side of the path, giving the attacker an opportunity to escape.

As she stared at the rubble, Julia didn't, at first, hear the noise. A crying sound, like that of a small child. When it did register, she frowned and tried to identify the direction. A path entered the woods and the crying seemed to get louder as she moved farther and farther into the trees.

Tap-tap.

Tap-tap.

The secondary, hammer-like sound took a moment to make sense of. Maybe the villagers were working on something? But why didn't they hear the crying?

Intent on triangulating the direction, she missed the insistent rustling until it grew to a roar. Until she looked up.

Pop! Pop! Pop! Branches moved in time with the onslaught of a giant tree falling directly toward her.

Oh, shit!

There were only two things that Julia could do. Scream or run for her life. She did them both. Every ounce of strength raced into overdrive. Yet it seemed more like a slow motion scene.

Blood pounded in her ears.

Boom-boom. Boom-boom. Boom-boom.

Her feet pounded across the dirt in perfect time, arms pumping away to increase her momentum.

Boom-boom. Boom-boom. Boom-boom.

The veins in her neck stretched out as if that extra inch would help her get across the finish line faster.

Boom-boom. Boom-boom.

Julia outran the height of the tree. But not the width, and the branch that caught her opened a bloody trail down her arm and tossed her to the ground.

Her head hit and then, nothing.

The scream sliced through him like a frigid wind, followed by the crackling duel of branches as a tree fell. Hawk barely felt the tremor as it hit. He was already on the run.

The shriek belonged to Julia.

He beat the other men by at least two minutes and found her working futilely to free herself from the branches of a downed tree.

"Hawk!" Julia cried with relief. "Thank God. Get me out of here! We've got to help that child."

He closed his eyes, just for a moment, and gave thanks that she was alive. Her words sunk in about the time he started heaving brush out of the way. "What child?"

"The one in the woods. I heard a child crying. That's why I came up here." She pushed on the limb she was stuck under. "I'm pinned down. You've got to get me out."

Manuel and the other villagers arrived and Hawk sent them in search of the child. "Lie still," he said. "You could be hurt."

"Well, of course I'm hurt. A damn tree just fell on me."

He grunted, tossing a limb aside that would have challenged anyone else, yet he made it look like a match stick.

Julia struggled to sit up, but Hawk restrained her with a hand to her shoulder.

"We've got to find that child," she said.

"I've sent Manuel and the men to look. You don't move until I know you're all right."

For once she accepted his order with grace. He sent a quick thank you skyward as he checked her for injuries. He began at the top, carefully feeling for the lump where her head had connected with the ground.

"Ouch!"

"You've got an egg there, but no open wound. That's good. Did you black out?"

"Umm, no. I don't think so." Julia brushed dirt off her arms.

She was lying. He was almost sure of it, but he let it go. He moved to her arms, unable to keep from noticing how nicely muscled they were. The woman worked out. Lifting the arm torn up by the branch, he bent it at the elbow. "Any pain?"

"No, other than a burning sensation from the scrape."

"It's more than a scrape. We'll need to get some antiseptic on it as soon as possible."

He moved on to her abdomen then. Nice and firm. His hands faltered as he palpated for any pain.

Julia squirmed beneath him.

Focus, man. Hawk looked up. No abdominal injuries, if the scathing look on her face was any indication.

He checked legs that distracted him beyond reason, feeling along the calf muscle, looking for tender spots or open wounds. His hands lingered. Everything else faded as he continued. She had nice legs. Shapely and very, very sexy. He ran his hands over them slowly, gaining familiarity with the smooth, soft skin. Feelings he strove hard to deny stirred again. Intimate feelings. He'd like to run his hands along her skin, all the way to—

"A-hem?"

He felt the heat hit his face and grunted at the realization he'd been caught in the act. Hawk quickly moved on to trace a path along the bottom of her feet. She twitched.

He smiled, his confidence righting itself. "Ticklish?"

"You think?" she shot back. "Are you done feeling me up now? Can I please get up?"

His eyes flared. "Trust me, counselor. If I were feeling you up, as you so eloquently put it, you wouldn't want to get up."

The flush in her cheeks deepened and Hawk smiled to himself at the knowledge that he could disconcert this tiger so easily.

He helped her to stand as the men returned. Manuel explained that they found no child, but he would return to the village to make sure all were accounted for. Hawk relayed the information to Julia, who wilted against his side. He swung her up in his arms, then asked the rest of the men to check the tree. He would take the senorita back to the village.

God forgive him, but she felt good in his arms.

"Put me down," she said in a low, urgent voice.

He detected a slight shudder and smiled. "Worried, counselor?"

She looked beautiful even angry. Oh, yes, she was affected. The realization made his smile broaden.

"Hawk, I'm fine. I can walk."

"Not this time."

"Please." Her eyes pleaded, all smoky blue and spiced with a tinge of indignation. They held his gaze for a moment, then turned away as a subtle change overcame them. Desire. In that moment, Hawk knew the meaning of infinity. He was lost. She desired him and he wanted her just as much. Maybe more. His gaze moved to tempting lips. Lips he knew wanted his kiss. He remembered last night, and the kiss that had already all but shattered his life.

He started and pulled his head back. No. This would not happen. He wouldn't let it. For Maria's sake. He steeled himself against the pain that he knew he would see in her eyes. Holding her tighter, he struck out for his hut.

Hawk poured antiseptic on the gauze and laid it against the scrape on her arm.

"Ow!"

"Uh, yeah, this might sting a little."

"No kidding."

"Stop squirming. I need to get this scrape cleaned up."

The sting eased and Julia tried to sit quietly through his ministrations. He was close, his head bent over his work. She could smell his hair, all wood smoke and handmade soap.

A warmth began to seep through her. She wanted very badly to lay her head on that shoulder. *So this is what it's like to be cared for.*

It felt safe. Comfortable. Sensual.

His touch was surprisingly gentle and the heat began to tingle and coalesce. She imagined those hands touching her in other ways, like she'd wanted them to back in the woods. He could have taken her then and there, and she would have welcomed it. Something pulled him up, most likely Maria. His devotion astounded Julia...and infuriated her. His wife had been dead for over a year. It was hard to compete with a ghost.

Move on, buddy. See what's right in front of you. Better yet, let me know what that devotion is like. Love me like you love her.

Julia froze. Never in her life had she used that word, except in relation to her mother. Ever. Now, here she was, close to swooning over some backwoods pirate.

This could not happen. She had places to go and promises to keep. He would not derail her plans.

A whiff of the fragrant flowers laced with his woodsy scent wound its way through, softening her heart again. She leaned in to rest her head on his shoulder, prepared to give in.

"I've arranged for a boat," Hawk said. "You're going home first thing in the morning."

Ice cold water doused the fire in her veins. "You what?"

"You heard me, counselor."

Yes. I heard. And I'm not leaving. "I can't."

"Can't what?" Hawk set the antiseptic down, looking everywhere except at her.

"Can't leave. I have to help you figure out what's going on."

"No, you don't."

"Hawk, you've tried to figure this out and haven't been able to. Even Dion has run into a brick wall."

"We'll get to the bottom of it."

"I can help."

"You..." Hawk ran both hands through his long hair and started over. He crouched in front of her and set his hands on her knees. "Your safety is distracting me. I can't focus."

Julia pressed the advantage. Lightly caressing his cheek, she was rewarded as he dipped his head toward hers.

"Are you sure it's just my safety that bothers you?"

Dion burst in. Hawk's head whipped up, and Julia dropped her hand.

"Things are escalating," Dion said without preamble.

"How?" Hawk asked.

"The tree that injured Julia didn't fall naturally. It was cut."

CHAPTER NINE

Hawk, Julia, Dion and Claire sat aboard the *Treasure* in somber silence. Dinner lay forgotten on their plates. Claire tried half-heartedly to nibble on a piece of fruit her husband handed her.

Julia voiced their biggest worry. "So whoever blasted the mud path isn't gone. Someone here in the village is still bent on sabotage."

Hawk was silent, but Dion answered her. "It seems that way. There was no child in the woods crying. Plus, that tree was cut to send it crashing in the direction you were drawn."

She shuddered. "And you have no idea who could be behind this?"

"No."

She turned to Hawk. "Is there anyone here who is new?"

He didn't answer right away. She could almost see his mind turning like a centrifuge. Maybe he was mentally running through the streets, searching for the answer. Or maybe he was looking for a way to protect from scrutiny the people he knew and loved. "I haven't seen anyone that I haven't known for my entire time here."

"Okay. Could one of the villagers be behind this?"

Hawk glared at her so she switched gears. "Can you think of anyone here who has a grudge against the village—or against you?"

"No."

"Come on, Hawk. No place is perfect. Every place has its dissidents."

"Not here!"

She put her hand up, giving Hawk a hard look. "All right. We'll assume for the moment it's not someone who lives here. That means it must be someone who doesn't live here."

"What do you mean?" Claire asked.

"You said you don't get many visitors here. Does that mean no one, or the rare visitor or two?"

"Apart from you, Julia, we haven't had outsiders here for several months. Oh!" Claire stood. "Except for your father, Hawk."

Julia whirled on Hawk in time to see him look away. He shifted in his seat as she waited for an explanation.

None was forthcoming. He sat in stony silence as they stared at him.

"Well?" Julia asked.

"Well, nothing," Hawk answered.

"It's not nothing. Your father was here?"

Hawk got up and began to pace. "Yes. But it has nothing to do with this."

"How do you know that?"

"Because." Hawk glared at her. "Because he came to see me, not the village."

Julia dredged up her best courtroom stare to counter his glower. "Does that mean you actually spoke to him?"

"Yes." One word, spoken with such venom, left no confusion about their relationship. He stopped at the railing and stared out across the small bay to the village beyond.

Apparently, the visit had caused Hawk a world of hurt. Julia's heart ached to take the sting away. She joined him. "What did he come for, Hawk?" She tried to convince him with her tone that she wanted to help, but she knew it didn't work when he slapped the railing.

"It's none of your business, counselor."

Disappointment washed through her like acid. He did not trust her enough to confide in her. "All right. You win. I won't ask again."

Julia turned her back to him and spoke to Dion. "If it's not someone in the village, someone is staying nearby and causing this damage."

Dion spoke then. "You've seen what it's like getting here by land. It's a maze of jungle. We could spend years trying to ferret out someone hiding out there." He waved toward the woods.

Claire picked up their untouched dishes and took them below, returning with a bottle of wine and three glasses. Handing them around, she gave voice to their worries. "So, we can't stop this?"

Hawk leaned against the rigging. "There has to be a way."

"I don't think we're finished yet," Julia said. "If we can't catch the culprit here, then we're back to the original question."

"Who is behind all of this?" Dion answered.

"Yes. What do we have?"

"Not much," Hawk said. "We know that someone is trying to keep this village from being rebuilt."

"That's for certain," Julia answered. "Who would want to do that?"

"I don't have a clue."

"Who wants this village to fail?" she said.

No one had an answer for that.

She tried again. "Who has a stake in this village?"

All three heads came up.

"What do you mean," Claire asked.

Julia stared at Hawk. "I mean that if someone doesn't want your village rebuilt, then whoever it is must have other plans for it."

Hawk and Dion jumped up at the same time. "Damn!" they said in unison. "How can we find out if—?"

"—someone has made inquiries into this area? I know someone," Dion finished.

"Finally! We have something to pursue."

It was the first time Julia saw actual satisfaction cross Hawk's face. Then, he looked at her, and it disappeared. The mask moved firmly back into place. He couldn't let her in. Or wouldn't. Either way, it hurt more than she wanted to acknowledge. She hung her head, so close to letting tears fall she had to get out of there.

"I should be going."

"Oh, Julia. We completely forgot. How is your head?"

She touched the tender area, more for effect than out of need. "Pounding a bit. I think it's time to call it a night."

"I'll take you back," Hawk said quietly.

Julia stiffened. "No need. I know the way. If you could get me ashore, though, I'd appreciate it. I don't feel much like a swim tonight."

The hugs and thank yous that followed had Julia barely holding it together. Somewhere in this mess that her life had become, she'd started to care what happened to Claire and

Dion, and to Tierra Bonita. And, God help her, to one Hakon Thoralssen II. He was a man who had mountains of strength, yet couldn't find the way beyond his grief. He couldn't let it go long enough to embrace love again.

Love? Julia mulled the word over during the ride to shore. Hawk's sure strokes with the oars only added effect.

Could she love Hawk? She didn't want to. Hell, she didn't have time to fall in love. But the man seemed to invade her mind. No, she corrected. Her heart. For the first time in her life, she felt helpless to resist the assault. She had fearlessly taken on the best attorneys in San Diego and beaten the majority of them. She'd defied her father by shacking up in Hawaii, then returned to grovel at his bedside, promising him anything, if he would just live another day.

And here she was, ready to throw away her promise over a man who appeared unable to lay his wife to rest.

Hawk helped her out of the skiff. He walked her to her room, never saying a word.

She turned at the door, staring at the ground. "You win, Hawk. I'll go home."

He reached for her, then stopped. God help him. He didn't want Julia to go. He wanted... Damn it. He wanted more than he had a right to ask. This woman had fought with him, and for him, ever since they'd met. Now she fought for his village. Maria's village.

He wasn't ready to let go of the past. Hell, he probably never would be. He couldn't give Julia what she wanted, what she needed.

He moved closer. Neither could he resist her.

Hawk touched her hair and shivers threaded his veins with heat. He felt the warmth flood his face and spread through his body until it lodged like a red-hot stake in his groin.

It seemed natural to caress her cheek.

Julia's arms were a barrier between them. Her head came up and his heart cracked at the unshed tears. Instinct took over as Hawk shut the door on yesterday and vowed, for now, to live in the moment. He leaned down and kissed lips that had invaded his dreams for days.

She pushed against him and held his gaze for one long, hard minute. Then, the barrier gave way. Her arms snaked their way around his head and pulled him down to renew the kiss.

She parted her lips and it was his undoing. Hawk responded with all the lust and emotion pent up within him since first setting eyes on her. He devoured her and she welcomed him with her response.

Somehow, they made it inside his hut to his bed. They shed their clothes and fell down into the feathered softness.

He wove strands of silky auburn hair around his fingers and lowered his mouth again to hers. She moved her hands over his body, her feather-light touches branding him wherever they made contact.

Hawk groaned as she followed the arc of his hip, then wound her way up his stomach. He stopped breathing when she circled his nipple and raked her nails through the hair on his chest.

He was rock hard, an exquisite torture he was not sure he could withstand. Drawing a ragged breath, he stilled her hand and began his own exploration.

He claimed her lips and she opened up to him with a lingering sigh. Her tongue found his and his groin twitched as he pulled her deeper. She tasted warm and fruity, and he lost himself in a tropical paradise of flavor.

He needed more and moved to cover her neck with his hand.

She shifted to give him room.

As his hand slid to her shoulder, her throaty moan voiced the loss of contact. It changed to a gasp as he peppered her skin with soft kisses. His fingers felt the tiny raised bumps along her arms as she reacted to his touch.

Continuing his exploration, his fingernails trailed up the underside of her arm. The incidental brush of her breast brought on another moan, only this time, it came from him.

Julia dug her fingers into his back as he claimed her, circling, backing off, then circling again. Her breast in his hand felt the perfect fit. Small, but not too small. And so very reactive. His thumb crossed over a hardened nipple, then he kissed his way slowly, languidly to the prize his hand held.

She arched her back, pleading.

Hawk backed slightly away.

And Julia groaned, trying to pull him back.

His lips grazed her breast and she shuddered. Hawk froze long enough to retain some minimal power over his out-of-control body. Then, he lowered his head and drew a nipple into his mouth, his cock jerking more as she arched her back further. The sweet agony in his groin made restraint all but impossible. It wouldn't take much.

Julia's hands had started to move again. She glided from his back to his arms, then found the line of hair on his stomach and followed it down...

Down.

And further down.

She grasped him and he groaned, releasing her breast as he moved to stop her.

"Give. Me. A. Moment."

"I don't need a moment. I need you. Inside me. Now," she said, her voice husky as she drove her hips against him.

He struggled to draw a breath, then reached down to swirl his tongue around each nipple before he raised himself over her.

He thrust into her. And she welcomed him.

She gasped as he filled her, then matched his rhythm and he felt her give herself completely to the sensations. He didn't hurry. He drove her to the edge, then backed off. Then took her to the edge again.

His hand move between them and he found her with his fingers, finally sending her over the precipice on a long, rolling ride.

He was more than ready and joined her in one final, climactic thrust.

Hawk howled his pleasure.

And, by the smile on Julia's face, he knew that she didn't give a damn who heard.

Julia snuggled deeper into Hawk's side as she slept, and he smiled and held her close just as the moon slipped into perfect position to lighten the inside of his hut.

Hawk turned to the empty wall where Maria's picture used to hang. He'd removed it when he'd brought Julia here unconscious, using the logic that he didn't want her to know it was his home she stayed in.

Acid chewed his stomach into mincemeat as the past came crashing back in, and it took every ounce of his strength to stay still and not startle Julia out of her slumber.

What have I done? Guilt washed over him like a tempest as he started to shake.

"I'm sorry," he mouthed to the empty wall. "You deserve so much better than this betrayal."

There'd been other women in his life, but none since Maria. He'd thought those days behind him until tonight. He thought of her, tried to picture her. For one immeasurable moment in time, the only image that came to mind was of dark, auburn hair and a smattering of freckles.

He couldn't breathe. His heart pounded like a sonic boom and the room darkened around him as if a cloud obscured the moon. He lay there in a deep sweat.

Maria! He almost shouted the name.

He needed out. With slow desperation, Hawk extricated himself from Julia and pulled a sheet carefully up to her neck.

Opening the bottom drawer of his bureau, he pulled out the picture, gazed at it for long seconds, then held it to his chest as if it would still his heart. "I'm so sorry," he said to the picture.

He set the picture on top of the chest and crossed to the bed. "I'm sorry," he whispered. Then, he turned and left the hut.

Julia watched him slip out of the room. She clutched the sheet to her and curled tightly into a ball, feeling his warmth still clinging to the bed, his woodsy scent still on the pillow. One lone tear escaped.

"I love you," she said to the empty room.

CHAPTER TEN

Hawk made his way back down to the beach, surprised to see Dion pacing back and forth.

He didn't waste time with niceties. "I've been out at the tree that fell. I wanted to get some pictures of the cut ends."

"For evidence," Hawk said.

"Yes. Not that it will help. The man-made cut is pretty damn evident. Tomorrow, I'll radio my friend Aidan in England and ask him to make some inquiries."

"Thanks."

Dion picked up a pebble and launched it out into the water. "Um, Hawk?"

"What?"

"I think you need to go back with her tomorrow."

Hawk's head came up. "No."

"We need someone in San Diego."

"There's no reason for me to be there. I need to be here. "

"There are a lot of reasons, and you know it. First, I need to give Aidan a contact phone number."

"We can do it from here," Hawk said.

"What am I going to do? Tell him to radio at a certain time and stand by waiting? I think you know that won't work. It's time-consuming, the reception is bad and it's not exactly private." Dion paused a moment before plunging ahead. "There's a bigger reason."

Hawk squirmed.

"First, I need to ask you a question." He nodded his head toward the village. "What's going on with you two, anyhow?"

"Nothing." Hawk's chest hurt as he told the lie.

"Look, it's obvious you are attracted to each other. What's holding you back?"

Unable to stand the ache any longer, Hawk turned to stare out across the water. "I'm married."

Dion's arm clamped down on his shoulder. "I think, my friend, that you are in love with two women. And sooner or later, you're going to have to let one of them go."

Hawk curled his hands into tight fists. "Stay out of it."

For a moment, Dion looked like he would pursue it. Hawk was ready to deck him if he did. This was not a conversation they were going to have. Hell, he hadn't even settled it with himself yet.

"Here's the bottom line," Dion said. "It's obvious that whoever is behind this knows of Julia's involvement. That noise, that child crying? Someone drew her into those woods. She needs protection."

The thought of something happening to Julia filled Hawk's gut with lead. If he stayed here, he would be helpless to keep her safe. It was the mudslide all over again. There was nothing he could do, at least not from here. Taking a deep breath, he gave Dion the only answer he could. "Point taken. I'll think about it."

"That's all I ask." Dion looked as if he planned to say more but thought better of it.

Smart man.

Instead, he patted Hawk's shoulder again and turned away. "'Night." He waded into the water for the quick swim home.

Hawk watched him go, his mind trying to unravel the plot that seemed to be whirling around him. First, there were the disruptions here in the village. Then, Julia became embroiled in it when someone posted his bail using her name. That had happened in San Diego. Now, this attempt on her life escalated things.

Julia. Emotions coursed through him that he'd shut out for so long. Emotions he didn't want and could no longer stop. And now she was in danger because of him.

Hawk picked up a stick and stabbed it at the sand. Who the hell was behind all this? His father? As ruthless as his father was, he could not imagine him ordering the destruction of a village. He thought of Julia's brush with the tree and what could have happened.

Could his father be capable of that?

The day his father arrived in Tierra Bonita had been one of the lowest points in Hawk's life. Still reeling from Maria's death, he'd failed at every attempt to raise capital for the reconstruction. He'd spent two long months stateside soliciting donations. He'd asked, demanded, even begged. It was as if he'd been blackballed. Every philanthropic organization, every corporate deity he'd met with had refused to help. He'd been back in the village less than a week when the yacht had rounded the promontory and anchored in the bay.

Finally, he thought. Someone had taken notice. Sending praise skyward for the help, Hawk rowed out to the boat. Its name even seemed appropriate. *Touch of Gold*.

"Ahoy, the yacht," he called out as he pulled alongside.

He was welcomed aboard and taken to a salon that rivaled Dubai for decadence. Wall panels covered in what looked like golden cloth offset ivory carpet that showed no signs of wear or use. Not even a vacuum line. Hawk ran his hand along a chair. The gold and brown leather was the softest he'd ever felt. Deep cherry wood and gleaming brass spoke the language of money. A lot of money.

Whoever owned this boat would rival his father for wealth.

"Hello, son."

Hawk stiffened. Shit. He did not need this. It figured his father would make this sort of entrance. Tension-coiled muscles relaxed by will alone as he affected a nonchalant posture and turned to greet the elder Thoralssen. "Dad. How nice to see you." His tone dripped with a barbed honey.

Hakon Thoralssen I ignored the comment. "You're a hard man to track down," he said as he poured a glass of his favorite scotch. Chivas Regal was the only palatable scotch whisky made, according to his father. Hawk shook his head. The cost of that bottle alone would go a long way toward renovations.

"Would you care for a glass?"

"No thanks, Dad."

The elder Thoralssen's eyes narrowed. "I've asked you to call me Father. Or Hakon, if you wish."

"I know, Dad. So, are you here to donate to the cause?"

"What cause?" He waved his hand toward the salon window. "You mean this village you've spent the last few months stumping to raise funds for?"

Hawk could feel the red creeping up his neck and clamped his hands to his side to keep from doing something he might regret. "Yes, Father. I mean this village. Are you contributing to the renovations?"

"No."

The warmth in his face started to boil. "Why not?"

"Because it's a waste of money."

"I do not agree with you," he said through clenched teeth. He dared not relax or they would start to sputter a long held anger. "So, then, to what...or whom...do I owe this honor? Is there a purpose to your visit?"

"Can't a father simply wish to see his son?"

"Most fathers could. You, however, never do anything without a motive."

"Hmm." Hakon smiled. "You always did know how to cut to the chase." He took a sip of scotch. "Have it your way. I've come to bring you home from this hovel you've adopted as some sort of pet project. This village of yours is a shabby use of what appears to be prime space. It's time to be done with it. And for you to stop shirking your duties and assume your position within Thoralssen Industries."

Crimson rage engulfed Hawk and the room around him took on a ruby-colored hue. He walked with slow, careful steps until he was within arm's reach of his father, taking a long moment to stare into ice blue eyes that mirrored his own. Taking the drink out of Hakon Thoralssen's hands, he downed the amber liquid, then slammed the glass down on the polished cherry wood bar. Droplets of scotch lit everywhere.

"I will never, ever work for a company as cruel and shameless as yours. Ever."

He turned to walk out. As he opened the door to leave, his father lobbed his parting shot. "If you walk out of here, Hakon, there is no more us. You will be disinherited."

Hawk laughed. "Finally, I can get a good night's sleep. Good to see you, as always, Dad."

Hawk had rowed back to shore and paced the beach, filled with a furious wrath that he could find no containment for, unable to fathom his father's egotistical agenda. The man was insane to think he could come here and bring Hawk back. Hell, the man didn't know what the word home even meant!

Hawk watched as the yacht weighed anchor. Hakon Thoralssen I lived in luxury on board while the people Hawk called family slept in shelters and tents and worried daily what they would eat.

That yacht would go a long way to feeding these people.

He squinted at the departing boat. Selling a boat like that would help a lot.

He watched the *Touch of Gold* until it disappeared from sight, formulating a plan in his mind. Then, his anger waned while walking back to the main part of the village, and he began to whistle. He finally had a way to help.

Thanks, Dad.

Sitting on the beach now, Hawk tossed the stick in a high arc into the water and watched it splash, then send ever-widening circular ripples rolling outward. That night, with his father, a pirate had been born. Hawk had done what he needed to do for Tierra Bonita and he refused to regret it. It had helped, but not enough. Now, again, as he was poised to see his dreams happen, someone lurked nearby, bent on destroying them. No matter what he thought of dear old dad, he doubted even *he* would stoop to this level of deception.

The next morning Hawk walked to his hut filled with dread. A bad night's sleep on the beach didn't help his disposition. He'd delayed as long as he could, but the water taxi had been in the harbor for half an hour. It was time to go.

His knock yielded a terse "come in."

The picture of Maria lay untouched where he'd left it. Julia sat on the bed, hands folded in her lap, her suitcase packed and ready beside her.

"Julia—"

"Is the boat here?"

"Yes. About last night," he said.

She interrupted him. "Great. I'm ready to go."

"We need to talk," he tried again.

"No, Mr. Thoralssen, we don't. Not if it's about last night. Believe me, I'm as sorry as you are about what happened."

Hawk flinched as the words hit him like a left jab. She'd heard his apology.

"I'm an attorney. You're my client. That's all there can be between us." Cold eyes stared him down. "Last night *never* happened."

"We can't deny it."

"Oh, yes, we can. And you will. My professional reputation is at stake here." Julia lowered her voice. "You owe me this."

Hawk's lips compressed as he searched for a reason to refute her statement. She was right. He couldn't give her anything more, so the least he could do was keep quiet. But he sure as hell didn't have to like it. He ground out a "fine" and turned to let her lead the way out, reaching for his duffle as they left.

Hawk tried to take her bag from her.

"I've got it," she said.

They didn't speak to each other. They couldn't even if they wanted to. The village seemed to have come out en masse to say goodbye to Julia. It was a long, slow, agonizing walk to the dock. More than once he watched Julia's eyes fill with tears as someone hugged her or handed her a flower.

Mama Rosa handed her a small bag. "A little food to help you on your journey." She gave Julia a kiss on each cheek and a hug that Julia returned tightly. Releasing her, Mama patted her cheek. "You will always have a home her, mi hija. You are one of us now."

Tears trickled down Julia's face as she answered. "Thank you. It's...an honor to be so welcomed here."

Hawk helped Julia into the boat and stowed her suitcase and his duffle. She didn't notice when he settled beside her, probably because her gaze remained on the group of people still waving goodbye. He released the rope that held them to the dock, and the boat drifted out.

"What are you doing?" Julia asked.

He didn't even try to pretend. "I'm going with you."

"Oh, no, you're not." She stood up, almost tipping the small boat over as her flowers spilled to the deck. "Oh, no!" She dropped to her knees and picked up one flower at a time. He watched the care she took to settle each blossom securely in her other hand before going after the next one.

Her tears surprised him as she settled back on the bench and ran her hands along the stems.

"You can't go home with me," she said, the quaver in her voice noticeable only to him.

He tried to lighten the mood. "First, you try to drag me back. Now you don't want me anywhere near San Diego?"

Still-damp eyes glared at him.

"Trust me," he said. "If there were any way around it, I'd take it. But you were right. We need to work together on this."

"I can handle my end of things just fine."

The thin line of Hawk's lips hardly qualified as a smile, but it was the best he could do. "Of that, I have no doubt, counselor. But you need my knowledge of the situation. Besides, there's the attempt on your life to think about."

Her eyes widened. "My life? How do you know they were after me?"

"We don't. Not for certain. Until we do, someone has to keep you safe."

"And you've done such a good job of that so far," she spat.

Hawk crooked his head in acknowledgement.

"I can take care of myself," Julia said.

He used her own words against her. "Yes. You've done such a good job of that so far."

Julia glared at him.

"I'm not going to change my mind. I'm going with you. Look at it this way. With your savvy and my knowledge, we should be able to get to the bottom of this in no time. The sooner we solve this riddle, the sooner I'm out of your life."

He watched the lines of her jaw retract, then relax as she relented. "A valid argument. You win."

The boat got them as far as Acapulco. Hawk ordered her a cab and then left her on the dock with a vague "I'll see you in San Diego." Julia watched him walk off, knowing that the chance, however little, of any sort of relationship with him had been left far behind in an idyllic little village.

She glanced down at her cell phone and her melancholy fled when she saw coverage bars colored in.

"Finally," she muttered as she dialed her office.

"Stanski, Rawlins, and Benton. Julia Branholt's office."

"Gail. It's me."

"You shit!" Gail began. "Where the hell have you been?"

"I told you. In Mexico. And I'm still here."

"For this long? I've been dodging questions like crazy! You owe me big, girlfriend."

"And then some. And I'm going to owe you even more."

Julia heard the sigh on the other end of the phone. She hung her head, aware of what she was asking of her assistant... No, that wasn't right. Gail was her friend, and Julia knew full well what she now involved her in. There wasn't much of a choice.

"I need your help," Julia said.

"Are you all right?"

"Yes. For now. I can't explain until I get home."

Gail hesitated on the other end of the phone. It didn't take long. "What can I do?"

"Check into a few things for me. First of all, Tierra Bonita del Dios."

"The village in Mexico?"

"Yes. I need to see if anyone has been making inquiries into the land there..." Julia laid out her list of things to research and was relieved when Gail took it all in stride. She didn't deserve such a good friend. Gail would make sure she paid her back, though. Probably by drawing her out to yet another meat-market, a.k.a. dance club. The thought brought a smile to her face.

As it turned out, that was the highlight of her day. Julia made it to the airport only to find out she'd missed the last possible flight bound for home. Standing at the counter as she booked a flight for the next day, Julia cursed the noise abatement rules that closed down late-night flights into San Diego. She looked around at the uncomfortable plastic airport seats and asked the attendant for the phone number to the closest hotel.

An hour later she tossed a salad-to-go on the desk and took advantage of one of the modern conveniences she'd missed the most—a hot shower. Lukewarm on a good day had been the best Tierra Bonita could do, along with marginal privacy in the communal showers. She shook her head. Still, the village and its people, had somehow wound their way into her heart.

Julia stood under the steamy spray for a long time, hoping the water would wash away the sense of foreboding that seemed to have settled in her soul. Where was Hawk? And how would he get across the border? He hadn't bothered to let her in on that secret. She let the spray rain over her. There were a lot of things he'd never bothered to let her in on, his heart at the top of the list.

Finally, she turned the water off and reached for a towel. She opened a bottled water and took a sip, the salad no longer holding any appeal. Curling up in a ball on the king-size bed, Julia ran her hand along the other pillow.

Somewhere, in this mess her life had become, she'd fallen in love with a pirate.

Late the next afternoon, Julia pushed the button for her floor and wilted against the elevator wall, her bag sagging to the ground. She was almost home. It seemed like ages since she'd last been home. In reality, only a few days had passed.

Days spent completely outside her urban comfort zone. Days spent learning to see beyond her world. Days spent falling in love with a village, and a pirate who would not let go of his past long enough to even glimpse a future.

Julia's eyelids fluttered closed as grief returned with a vengeance, weaving an aching trail through her heart and leaving daggers of regret in its wake. She pressed her fists over her chest to still the crescendo.

But there were no pounding beats.

Nothing spiked or crashed. She spread her fingers out and let the normal rhythm calm her.

Thump-thump.

Thump-thump.

The daggers were imaginary. Julia released a long, deep breath. Grief was toying with her. She patted her chest and forced the pain to a far corner of her heart. "I haven't got time for you. Please. Go away."

The elevator bells chimed. Julia stood straight and smoothed her wrinkled khakis as the doors to her floor opened. Juggling her suitcase as she navigated the familiar muted but modern hallway, Julia dug for keys relegated by disuse to the bottom of her purse.

Then, her steps faltered.

Hawk said he'd meet her here. He could be around the corner, sitting on the floor next to her door, wondering when she would get in. Just like in the movies.

His grin would take her breath away. She'd smile back, remembering his touch, his gentleness. She would ache to feel his arms around her again.

He would hold out his arms, and she would step into them, forgetting his regret that he'd made love to her. And forgetting that he couldn't let go of his late wife. In fact, she'd forget everything but the feel of him.

Grief screamed out of the box and Julia welcomed it, just for a moment. Long enough to right her world. "Go away," she whispered, sending it back to the nether regions of her mind.

She inched along the wall and peeked around the corner to her apartment door.

No one waited there.

Julia's shoulders stooped under the awareness of how badly she'd wanted him to be there. Instead, the back of her neck tingled.

He *is* here.

Her eyes flew open and stared directly into startled...hazel eyes? The eyes coalesced into the face of her next-door neighbor.

"Are you all right?" Josh Meier asked, a look of concern on his face.

"Yes." Julia prayed her time in the sun hid the rush of color to her face. She brushed her hair back, grasped her suitcase tighter, and moved away from the wall.

"Yes," she said more firmly. "I'm fine."

"You looked a little unsteady there for a moment."

"I was just..." The words trailed off. She had no excuse. "...in another world." She turned the corner, and Josh fell in beside her, passing his own door. She glanced down at her keys. "Really, Josh, I'm okay."

"I know. Just making sure."

Neighbors for a couple years now, they'd borrowed eggs, corkscrews, discussed condo association affairs, but never anything personal. Still, she'd never known him to be at a loss for words.

Josh was a good-looking guy. He had brown hair, a strong face, and nice eyes that trendy glasses didn't disguise. He was tall, but not too tall. Yes, Josh Meier had everything packaged the right way. A bit too much of the playboy with the women, though, if the changing of the guard from blonde to brunette, and back to blonde again was any indication.

She'd never known him to hesitate around any woman.

A sparkle in his eyes belied any sense of nervousness. "I wondered if you'd like to go to the ballet with me? I have tickets for tomorrow night."

Julia's eyebrows rose fractionally. He'd never so much as flirted with her. And she'd never felt a single spark for him. Or anyone else since she'd moved to San Diego. Maybe her career didn't keep her warm at night, but it did satisfy her desires.

At least, it had until she fell for an oversized Robin Hood with a morbid loyalty to a wife who could never return.

Julia caught herself before she shook her head. Donning her best I've-got-some-bad-news smile, she spoke. "Josh, I'm sorry. I just got back from a trip and I've got a million things to catch up on, both at home and at the office."

"You were south of the border, right?"

Julia frowned. "How did you know?"

He looked down briefly. "You're more tanned than before."

"Ah."

"And the papers mentioned that your client sailed into oblivion."

Julia's stomach tossed acid into her throat with the ease of a flame-thrower. Fighting for composure, she planted her best courtroom visage firmly in place and dusted off her disdainful cross-examination voice.

"What do you mean, my client?"

"That pirate," Josh answered. "Uh, you are defending him, right?"

"How would you know that?"

"It's been all over the papers."

That acid in her throat burned a hole to her lungs, letting caustic air turn her mouth into an arid wasteland.

"Exactly what are the papers saying?"

"Well, that you're representing him. That he's out on bail you posted—"

Shit.

"And that you've both disappeared." His smile broadened.

And there it was. Public opinion threw her in with Hawk without the benefit of a trial. And that meant the partners in her firm had done the same. Damn it all to hell. She was screwed. Professionally and personally. Damn. Damn. Damn.

"So," Josh continued. "If not the ballet, then some other time?"

"Josh," Julia said bluntly, "in two years you've never indicated any interest in me. Why now?"

"I don't know." He shrugged and stared at her like she was some muscle car churning out throaty roars in anticipation of the race. "It's different now. Kind of...exciting."

Josh all but forgotten, Julia closed the door behind her and, this time, fought the urge to let it hold her up. The press had branded her. She was in cahoots with Hawk. At least, she was according to the journalists and, most likely, the general population. Her law firm probably thought the same. Innocent until proven guilty didn't count when the reputation of a prestigious firm was at stake. She didn't have a prayer of convincing the partners that she'd maintained the boundaries of legal propriety.

The fact that she crossed those boundaries didn't make things any easier. In fact, she'd exceeded them with all the panache of an Olympic swimmer who takes the gold, then is forced to admit to performance- enhancing drugs.

She'd slept with her client.

Her keys hit the side table with a wood-scratching skid as she strode into her living room. Her bag landed on the couch with a plop, and Julia plunked down beside it.

The stakes just graduated to about a nine point nine on the Richter scale. It wasn't just a matter of getting her client the best deal anymore, or even of finding out who'd sabotaged Tierra Bonita. Her professional reputation, everything she'd spent the last eight years working for night and day, week after weekend, was about to be demoted to amoeba-rank under the crushing feet of the partners of Stanski, Rawlins, and Benton.

Bam! Bam! Bam!

Julia stopped breathing as her heart hit her throat. Before her conscious mind could register movement, she was up, over and cowering behind the couch, her mind back in the forest, a giant tree falling everywhere around her, trapping her...

Bam! Bam! Bam!

Then, she heard a muffled voice. "Julia!"

Her door! Someone was pounding on her door.

As she pushed off the couch, Julia's arm screamed a painful reminder of her recent brush with the tree. She reached for the bandage and felt the dampness. It was starting to seep again.

"Julia, I know you're in there. Open the door!" The pounding began again in earnest.

Julia opened the door to a startled Paul Benton, his hand about to land another blow to the wood. He caught himself before falling forward onto his face. With a deep scowl, he muttered, "About time" as he strode past her.

"Come on in, Paul. Please." Julia shook her head as she waved him in behind his back and shut the door.

This was the last thing she needed right now.

"What in the hell are you doing?" He turned on her.

With a smile that mimicked the beauty contestant who'd taken second place, Julia walked past him and into the kitchen. "I'm fine, Paul. And how are you? The wife and kids doing well? Can I get you something to drink?"

The pinkish sheen to his face deepened to an unusual shade of red. Julia smothered a grim smile of satisfaction. She got two glasses of water and handed one to him on her way back to the living room.

"Drink some water, Paul. You look like you're going to stroke out."

"I damn well am! What the hell were you thinking, traipsing off after that pirate? And kissing him in broad daylight? Are you trying to completely destroy your professional career?"

He all but shrieked the last words, but Julia couldn't hear them for the roar in her own ears. Kiss? In public? "What are you talking about, Paul?" she asked, glad the shake in her voice seemed barely noticeable.

"I'm talking about this!" He thrust a newspaper article in her face.

She took it, but already knew what it showed. The parking lot of the jail where she'd lost complete control of her senses under the onslaught of Hawk's kiss. Even now, her body tingled with the memory.

And her hands shook with the ramifications as she set the newspaper down. No wonder her neighbor wanted to date her and her bosses wanted blood.

It had happened. Unable to refute it, she stood silent.

"Do you know how many rules you've broken?"

"Would those be the spoken ones or the unspoken ones, Paul?" The tremor in her voice disappeared as her courtroom personality kicked in. "Because I'm getting a little confused. You tell me to win cases in order to advance. I do. And I get passed over. You tell me to increase my billable hours. I do, even though you pile pro bono case after case on my desk. And still, I get passed over for partner."

"Partner is the least of your worries."

"What the hell do you mean?"

"You'll be lucky to practice law when the firm gets done with you. They're talking prosecution!"

Julia began to tap her fingers on the back of the couch. "Now, why would the firm be out to take legal action against me? I haven't broken any laws." She cringed inwardly as the naked form of her client above her in bed darted through her mind.

"Primarily, it's the ethics issue. Your contract states that is enough grounds for dismissal. Did you even read it?"

"I know my contract. There is no proof of any ethics violation." Julia looked closely at Paul.

His eyes shifted to the glass of water in his hand.

"Or do you think there is?" she asked.

He stood then, tall and ramrod stiff. "I wouldn't know. I wasn't called into the meeting. But mark my words, Julia, they'll find the evidence they need. They don't lose. Ever."

He set the glass on the coffee table and threw his hands up in the air. "It's not enough that you involve yourself in this mess. You've gone and involved your secretary, too?"

"Assistant, Paul. Gail is my assistant."

"Whatever." He waved. "She's an unemployed assistant now."

"Oh, no!" Julia's smile turned to horror as tears filled her eyes. "You—" She fought to keep them from spilling over. "You fired Gail?"

"We didn't have much of a choice now, did we?" He held up a manila envelope. "You had her working on research that has nothing to do with your job."

Any remaining tears evaporated as Julia let go of the couch and reached for the envelope, but Paul held it beyond her reach.

"Uh uh. This isn't yours."

"If that's the information Gail found, then it *is* mine. My client deserves the best defense possible. Now hand it over."

"That pirate stole yachts from some of our most prominent clients. He is a loser who deserves to be in jail."

That was it. Tired and in dire need of a life-cleansing shower, Julia'd had quite enough of her sleazeball advisor's pompous attitude.

"That pirate, as you call him, has more moral fiber in one strand of arm hair than you do in that whole dippity-do head of yours, Slick."

It took her only one step forward for Paul Benton to back away.

"Get out. Now. And you can tell the partners that I will answer all of their questions when I get into the office."

Julia took another step forward, and didn't bother to hide her smile as her advisor turned tail and scurried out the front door without so much as a by your leave.

Julia followed more slowly. This case was going to be her downfall. Everything she'd worked so hard for these last eight years was doing a drain-dive. How was she ever going to get out of this?

She reached out and flipped the deadlock on her door. At that instant, the French doors to her office burst open.

Julia whirled around. Grabbing the umbrella leaning against the wall, she swung it up as protection.

Strong fingers grasped her arm before she could complete her swing.

"It's me, Julia."

"Hawk!"

Julia stared at Hawk, then wilted into his arms.

"Damn you, Hakon Thoralssen. You've ruined me."

When Julia's boss entered the apartment and started to tear her apart, Hawk had listened with barely contained fury. He backed off to the other side of the office, only to swiftly cross back to the doors. He wanted to rip them off their hinges and beat the man to a pulp for talking to Julia like some flunky.

He knew Julia would never appreciate his interference, though. So he stayed in the office, waiting and listening. He had to admit, she didn't let the jerk get the best of her. He had only his own experiences with her in a courtroom to go by, but some day he'd like to see her argue a case in full tiger mode. Remembering her response to him in bed, he smiled. She was a tiger all right, and not just in the courtroom.

He ran fingers through his hair, clasped his hands behind his head, and moved again to the far side of the office and back.

He sat down at her desk. Moments later, he was back at the door.

Finally, he heard the words he'd been waiting for. *Get out.*

Already turning the handle of the office doors, Hawk forced himself to wait until he heard the front door close.

He whipped the door open and it crashed into the stop and reverberated with noise.

Hawk's rage fled as he saw Julia's reaction to his appearance. Her eyes reflected her recent brush with danger. Hell, the umbrella shook almost more than she did.

He watched as the feral look in her eyes dimmed, replaced by the sadness of a thousand dashed dreams.

He wanted to make it right for her. He just didn't know how. Even if he did, he couldn't help her until his own troubles were straightened out. Troubles that now affected her life, exactly as she said they would.

He held out his arms.

The umbrella hit the floor and Julia stared at him for a long moment before moving into his circle and mumbling about how he'd ruined her. She thumped him on the chest.

Once. Twice. And again.

Remorse chilled his soul, and he shivered as she shook in his arms. "I'm sorry, Julia. I'm so very sorry."

It didn't help him to say it. And it didn't seem to help Julia either. She had not yet raised her head. He couldn't stand her this way. So he did the only thing he could think of.

"You should never have followed me."

Her shaking stopped. Slowly, she pulled back out of his arms and looked up at him.

He felt cold.

"You're right," she said. "I did this to myself." She took a long, deep breath. "Make yourself at home. I'm going to bed."

He followed her to the hall and watched her enter what must be her bedroom, closing the door behind her with a soft click. He picked up the newspaper that had fallen on the floor and saw the picture of them, kissing, front and center.

Damn. He felt like a heel. Worse. Like Brutus sticking the knife into Caesar's back. The fight had gone out of her. Somehow, he needed to find a way to restore normalcy to her life. It was the least he could do. Hawk saw the whiskey bottle on the buffet and poured a shot, downing it in the hopes it would ease his guilt.

It didn't. Seeing Julia tonight shook him beyond his own comprehension. Confused, his mind carried him back to that day in the market of Oxaca when he'd seen Maria for the first time, bartering with the merchants.

Her shiny black hair fell in a braid down her back, and her eyes found joy in everything they saw. He'd been a goner, following her home to woo her, and a scant week later he had asked her father, Manuel, for his blessing. Manuel had requested that they wait six months. As village elder, he had that right. A small price to be sure of their love, he said. They waited. It almost did them in, but they honored his request. Being alone with her for the first time in six months, on their wedding night, he'd been afraid to touch her. Afraid of the strength of his love. Afraid the mirror would shatter and he'd be alone.

Hawk moved around the darkened room as it hit him. That same intensity had gut-punched him tonight when he'd opened her office door.

He loved her. He loved Julia.

Ah, Maria. How could this happen? I'm so, so sorry.

His life with Maria had been perfect. Now he seemed intent on throwing that away. No, he corrected. Not throwing it away. That would never happen. Maria was too deeply embedded in his heart.

He leaned back against the wall again and stared down the hall. Was there a place in his heart for both of them? Maria had his past. Could Julia be his future?

He felt the ache in his heart ease, like stitches bursting to let the pressure out. And grief gave one last sigh before releasing his heart.

Hawk wanted to rush down the hall, throw open the door and profess his love, but he stopped himself. She was pretty damn ticked off at him, and rightfully so. This was not the time.

He needed to convince her of the change in his heart. But how?

When no answers came, Hawk checked the door locks, then moved to the couch and sat down on the soft leather. San Diego was warm, but not as warm as Mexico. He patted the cool material and realized he didn't know where Julia kept her spare blankets.

He scrunched into an almost fetal position to get his frame to fit within the boundaries of the couch, his only pillow a small tuft of bolster.

It was going to be a long, cold night.

CHAPTER ELEVEN

Julia dialed her mother's phone number. "Hey, Mom."

"Julia! You're home?"

Guilt flooded Julia as she heard the relief in her mother's voice. "Yes. I'm sorry, Mom. I should have called you."

"To let me know you were going out of country? Yes, you should have."

"And to explain. I can't believe what the papers are saying." Her voice cracked. "It's not true, Mom. I'm not some criminal sidekick."

"Lordy, dear, you don't think I believe those gossip rags, do you?"

"I thought I should set the record straight."

"And so you shall. We'll have dinner and you can tell me all about it. You sound tired."

"I am. Bone tired."

After a pause that seemed to Julia to be filled with question marks, her mother continued. "Did your pirate come back with you?"

He's in my living room, Mom. I'm harboring a fugitive. Worse, I've fallen in love with him. "I'm...I really can't say." Julia cringed at the withheld truth. The relationship between them had always been one of honesty and discussion, not subterfuge.

Nothing about this situation felt right.

Not one damn thing.

After scheduling a dinner Julia didn't know if she could make it to, she set the phone in its cradle and stared at her bedroom door. Awareness of Hawk's presence on the other side left her antsy and unfocused. Her body screamed for sleep, but her mind and heart refused to listen.

A long, drawn out shower didn't help Julia. Neither did her comfy, curl-up-with-a-good-book pajamas. The brandy she thought would sooth her sat untouched on her dresser.

She paced back and forth between the window and her bathroom, skirting the bed each time. Julia rubbed her eyes. Her desperate need for sleep had been overruled by thoughts of Hawk. There were too many memories. She remembered the way his strong arms cocooned her so gently. She remembered the feral look in his eyes as tender had taken a back seat to passion, and how she'd met his thrusts with equal abandon.

Leaning against the window curtains, she stared out at the San Diego skyline without seeing it. She missed Hawk more than anything even though only a door separated them. Her head came up. He didn't have a blanket. In fact, she'd neglected to tell him it was a two-bedroom apartment. There was a spare room. Maybe...

She left her room and quietly opened the linen closet. Then, blanket in hand, she crept out to her living room. At the back of the couch she whispered his name. "Hawk?"

"Here."

The blanket slipped out of her hands. The deep, husky voice came from behind and resonated through her body, straight to her soul. Hands she couldn't seem to forget settled lightly on her shoulders, then traced unhurried lines down her arms to her wrists.

Julia sighed. Feather light caresses passed over her wrists and started up the inside of her arms.

Don't do this. It will only complicate matters further, her brain prompted, and she stiffened.

Hawk's hands stilled at the inner part of her elbow.

No, her heart cried. *Please don't stop.* Julia tried to turn in his arms.

"No," he whispered. "There will be no rushing this time."

"Hawk—"

"Shhh," he said into her ear, sending a shiver of desire straight through her. "Listen, love. We won't do this if you don't want to. It will stop right here. But somehow, I think you've missed me as much as I've missed you. And God," he groaned, "I have missed you more than I thought possible."

Julia knew she should run. He would hurt her. Hell, he already had. Right now, though, pain had been replaced by the intense torture of his touch. She wanted more than anything to find a release.

She wanted Hawk.

For always, if possible. For tonight, if that's all there could be.

She relaxed into him, heart pounding. "How can I miss you so much after so little time?"

Hawk's hands gripped her arms as his head dipped toward her neck and he kissed the hollow at its base. "I know exactly how you feel."

No, Julia thought. *You don't.* She shivered as his next kiss sent fuzzy tendrils of need through her body. All thought fled. She tried to reach for him, but his grip held her captive.

Hawk slipped her pajama top aside as he rained kisses on her neck and shoulders, sending ultra sensitive currents through her body. Each time, he brushed up against her hips. He was rock hard. And every touch felt like sweet burns sending hot bolts of need all the way to her soul.

Distracted by his sensual kisses, she didn't feel him release her until he began to unbutton her top. Slowly, agonizingly, he moved from button to button. Done, his hands wandered up the inside as he spread the material apart and cradled the underside of her breasts.

Yes. She arched her back, begging him to cover her. She needed more.

His thumbs briefly caressed her. She shuddered. Again, he lightly brushed her nipples. And a third time. They ached with need. She ached.

She reached between them and grasped him through his pants.

He gasped and loosed his hold.

Julia took advantage of the opportunity and turned in his arms. Looking into his face in the dim light, she smiled, reached for his hand and led him down the hall.

Eyes only for each other, they undressed, then met on their knees in the center of her bed.

Hawk cupped her face in his hands. "You are so beautiful, Julia."

He kissed her forehead, traced her eyes and cheeks with his fingers and lingered over her mouth. She leaned into his caress and smelled his now familiar smoky musk.

Hawk's head came down and he replaced his fingers with lips that had invaded many sleep-deprived moments.

She tasted whiskey and wanted to taste more. She ran her tongue over his lips, and he opened to taste her, pulling her hard against him, matching her need.

His hair brushed her cheek, and she reached up to bury her hands in the long strands.

But he pulled back. He guided her to the sheets and took several long moments to explore her body with his eyes. Julia paused. Did he see her? Or a ghost?

"I'm with you, Julia."

Barely able to breathe, she tried to speak, but Hawk placed fingers over her mouth.

"I need you to know," he said, "that there is no one else here in this room. Only you and I. I promise. I will never hurt you again."

Could she believe it? Dare she? Julia stared at him for what seemed like an eternity, and he waited. Finally, her lips moved, gently sucking his fingers inside her mouth. Releasing them, her hands reached up and balled into fists in his hair, pulling him down.

Just as their lips met, she whispered, "Love me, Hawk."

"I do," he whispered back.

The fire ignited anew, and what started as a tentative kiss quickly built in intensity. Julia ran her hands over a back rippled with muscles as Hawk left a trail of kisses from her lips to her neck and down to the dip between her breasts. She pushed into him with her body, craving contact.

But instead, he pulled back and reached for her hands. Placing them over her head, he captured them loosely in one of his large hands.

She understood. She could move at any time. She chose not to.

"You are so beautiful," he said, as he used his free hand to learn the curves of her body. He moved down one side and, barely touching her, across her hips.

Julia jumped as the almost non-existent contact made her quiver. She started to move into him, but his hand spread across her stomach, reminding her. *Don't move.*

"Is it your intention to drive me insane?"

He chuckled. "Very possibly." His hand crept up her stomach to the underside of her breast. She watched his eyes glow as her nipples hardened even further. She wanted his touch. Needed his touch.

His hand moved over her breast, across the dip and around the outside of the other one.

Julia couldn't help herself as a spasm ran through her. She arched her back. Before she could settle, he claimed her with his lips, which sent hot rivers of lava to her core.

Hawk groaned as he captured her breast in his mouth. His tongue played with her nipple, and she shivered again. Somehow, with her arms above her head, the intensity was heightened.

Not moving proved to be extremely hard to do. She wanted to touch him, to bring him the same pleasure he sent coursing through her. She started to pull her arms away just as his hand moved back to her belly.

And lower.

Skirting her hair, circling, caressing her thighs, pressing gently to separate them. She moved to meet his hand.

"Please," she begged.

And finally, he found her, making small circles that sent her spiraling into a long, rolling climax.

She reached for him and clutched him to her as the wave crested and passed. At that moment, all her promises coalesced into one: *I promise to love you forever.*

He held her for a long moment as she found her breath. Hawk held his own breath as Julia began to move her hands. She pushed him onto his back so she could explore. Digging fingers into his chest hair and pulling just a little, she sent twinges of pleasure through him. She followed up with kisses that made him go weak as she included both his nipples in her ministrations.

He gasped as her hand connected with him and he throbbed when she stroked him. He wasn't going to make it much further.

She must have sensed it. She raised herself over him and smiled. "Next time, I get to play longer."

She lowered herself onto him. Slowly, agonizingly, she began to move, leaning over him, offering him a taste of tantalizing breast. He pulled it into his mouth, kneading the other with his hand. Only for a second, though. He had no time left and took control of their rhythm. She moved with him, placing her hands on his chest for balance.

Together, they rode over the top and spiraled into the stars.

Moving a strand of auburn hair off her sleeping face, Hawk let the silky lock trail through his fingers. It was every bit as soft as he'd imagined during those long, tormented nights in jail. Nights when coal black hair and fiery auburn hair had played games with his mind. When desire and loyalty had shredded his heart. And thoughts of Maria had first become overshadowed with a new awakening.

He smiled, aware now that this was right. Julia had come to him for a reason. And Maria, who never let a day go by without living it fully, would be happy to see him move on with his life.

Hawk almost missed the sound. *Tap. Tap. Tap.* Someone was at the door. Julia didn't stir, so he rose carefully from the bed in the early dawn light and reached for his pants.

Gail tapped again on Julia's door, eyes focused on the hallway as she did so. Too much had happened over the past couple of days to be coincidence. And now she felt hyper vigilant—always glancing over her shoulder. She rubbed her arms for the hundredth time, trying to get her persistent case of goose bumps to disappear.

"Julia," she whispered furiously, head against the door. "It's me, Gail. Open up. Please!"

The door opened without preamble. She would have tumbled to the floor were it not for strong arms that blocked her fall. All she could see were bare, muscular arms that looked like they belonged to a linebacker.

Oh, crap. Breath froze in her lungs. They'd gotten to Julia! Gail wasted no time.

"Hai-ya!" she shouted. She attacked, kicking out with every bit of strength she could muster and hitting her mark dead center.

The man grunted, let loose and staggered back, falling to one knee. While he was down, Gail took full advantage, raining blows on his head, arms, any part of him she could reach. She shouted as she pounded him. "Julia! Where are you? Hurry!"

"Woman, stop hitting me or, by God, I'll return the favor," he growled.

She kept on until he pushed her off balance, grabbed both arms, and twisted them behind her back, planting her face against the wall.

Gail continued to struggle. She had to get to Julia.

"Stop it!" he barked.

Julia awoke to the commotion and ran to investigate. "What the hell is going on?" Julia asked as she rounded the corner, tying her robe. Sleep-filled eyes widened as she saw her friend up against the wall.

"Hawk, let go of her!"

"The woman damn near castrated me," he said without loosening his grip.

Julia reached out and tried to pry his hands away. "She's my friend, for crying out loud. Let. Her. Go."

With a final grunt of disgust, he slacked off. Glaring at Gail, he hobbled over and dropped onto the couch, pain and anger evident as he cupped himself protectively.

Gail watched him nervously and she tested her arms.

"You okay?" Julia asked her.

"Yeah. No thanks to him." She nodded toward the couch, which earned her another glare from Hawk.

Julia went over and rested a hand on his shoulder. "Are you all right?"

"I'll let you know."

"Okay. Well, I guess it's time for introductions then. Gail, I'd like you to meet Hakon Thoralssen II."

Gail blanched. "Th-this is your pirate?"

"Sure is."

"Oh, crap."

"That's an understatement. Care to tell us why you assaulted him?"

It was Gail's turn to slump into a chair. "I thought he was kidnapping you...or worse." She looked at Hawk. "I'm really sorry. If I'd known you were going to be here, I'd have never..." She squeezed her hands together one way, then the other as she turned to Julia. "You have no idea what the last couple of days have been like. The police searched your office and took your laptop. Then Paul Benton told me to pack up my desk when he found me doing research related to Tierra Bonita. Ever since then, I've had this nagging feeling that someone is following me."

Julia's eyes met Hawk's over Gail's head. This wasn't good. Paul had never mentioned the police to Julia during his tirade.

"I think we'd better start at the beginning," Julia said. She looked down at her robe and over at the man clad only in khaki cargo pants, unbuttoned at the top even, and she groaned inwardly. So much for no one knowing she'd slept with her client. Things were going from bad to worse.

"Let me make some coffee and change and we'll talk."

CHAPTER TWELVE

Dressed, Julia could handle anything. Adversaries, bad news—bring it on. Slipping into a pair of slimming black slacks and a gray knit turtleneck, she felt the old Julia starting to emerge. The Julia who didn't let anything stop her from getting answers, and who was on top of her game at every moment. Nothing sideswiped this Julia's agenda.

She checked herself in the mirror. No time for a shower or her normal routine. She'd have to settle for a ponytail and a light coat of mascara and lipstick.

She entered her kitchen and looked around at the cherry cabinets and stainless appliances with satisfaction. It felt good to be home. The deep, rich aroma of coffee permeated the air.

"Mmmmm. That smells wonderful. Thanks," Julia said to Gail, who was seated at the table rustling through the paperwork she'd brought. "Coffee is something I'm in dire need of this morning."

"No problem," Gail said, stifling a not-so-well-hidden smile. "You, um, look like you didn't get much sleep last night."

Julia chose to ignore her and rummaged around in the freezer. There wasn't much. A tin of cinnamon rolls and the whole grain bread she'd thrown in the freezer before heading out for Mexico.

Beggars couldn't be choosers and she was hungry. Ravenous, actually. Last night had been...well, it felt better than winning a huge case in court. Much better. She popped the rolls in the oven and set the bread out to thaw, thinking she hadn't, um, slept that well in a very long time. If ever.

"So," Gail started. "You and your pirate are getting pretty cozy."

The flush crept up Julia's neck inch by inch until her entire face felt like she was having a personal summer. She busied herself with plates, jam, butter and the other trimmings needed for breakfast and prayed her voice sounded steadier than the staccato she heard. "Not at all. He's simply staying here until his legal issues are resolved. It was the only way I could keep an eye on him," she finished, fully aware of how lame the excuse sounded.

Gail chortled with laughter. "Bull! Honey, anyone with even an ounce of intuition can see you two are smitten. And probably were a lot more than smitten last night!"

Julia whirled to make sure Hawk wasn't in the doorway. "Gail!"

Her friend stood and placed a hand on each of Julia's shoulders. "Look. I know there are risks here. But it's wonderful to see you focused on something other than work. It's been a long time coming. So stop worrying about it and just enjoy the moment, okay?"

Tears formed in Julia's eyes as Gail hugged her. "Ah, Gail. I've missed you."

"Mind if I join in the fun?" Hawk walked in, arms akimbo, apparently intent on making good on his request.

Just then, the oven timer went off.

"Too late," Julia said, turning to deal with the cinnamon rolls.

"Damn," Gail said.

Hawk wrapped Julia in an embrace. "It's good to see you laugh."

"Hawk, please," she said, squirming. "Gail's here."

He held on a moment longer, then let her off the hook.

"Coffee." He spun around. "I smell coffee." He poured himself a cup, then turned and leaned against the counter as if today was just like any other day.

Julia turned with the cinnamon rolls and almost dropped them as her mouth went slack. Fresh from a shower, Hawk's damp blond hair hung loose over a shirtless chest. Muscles rippled as he set his mug down and settled his hands on the counter behind him, which amplified the six-pack abs and trim waist. He'd put on his khaki shorts, thank God. Then she realized the top button was undone...again.

It took every ounce of strength Julia had to keep from dragging him back to her bedroom to rip those shorts off.

Julia remembered Gail and turned to her friend, who ogled Hawk with totally undisguised interest. Julia's libido beat a hasty retreat, and she slapped the cinnamon rolls on the table, causing them both to jump.

"Go put some clothes on, Hawk."

He grinned and left the room without comment.

Julia scowled at Gail. "Close your mouth. You look like an idiot."

Gail's eyebrows arched a couple notches as she reached for her coffee. "I wasn't the only one," she said.

Hawk returned moments later, pulling a T-shirt over his head as he joined them.

He turned a chair around backwards and sat down, reaching for a warm roll. Dabbing at the frosting that dripped from it, he looked up to see both women watching him. Gail smiled, but Julia's scowl was firmly in place. He grinned, then quizzed Gail, who appeared to be the lesser of two evils right now. "So, what's happened that has you kicking a man in the groin on first sight?"

That focused everyone, and Gail shuddered, turning to Julia. "It's been crazy since you left. Paul Benton started hounding me, asking if I'd heard from you. I never told him when you called, by the way. The slime doesn't deserve to know."

Hawk's blood began to boil all over again. "Yeah, Julia had a little run in with the esteemed Mr. Benton shortly after she got home last night."

"After you called, I began looking into what you asked me to." Gail shot a sideways glance at Hawk.

"It's okay," Julia said. "I've told Hawk what I asked you to research."

"Good. Anyhow, Benton stopped by my desk while I was out to lunch and found the envelope."

"Found?" Hawk asked.

"Yeah. Found. In my locked file cabinet, stuck in an un-related case file."

"How do you know it was Paul?" Julia asked.

"I caught him red-handed, the arrogant jerk. The file cabinet was open and he was standing there reading it."

"Why would Paul be digging through your files?" Julia asked.

"Because he's scum, that's why. And he knew he wouldn't get anything out of me." Gail got up and refilled her coffee. "At any rate, that's when he told me I was fired."

"I didn't know until last night. I'm so sorry, Gail. If I'd known—"

"Don't worry. I don't want to work there with jerks like him running the place."

"What reason did he give you?" Julia asked.

"He said I was using work time for personal research." Gail sat back down with a sigh.

"That's ridiculous! Hawk's case is still open."

"Yeah, but Tierra Bonita is not part of it. At least not according to Paul Benton."

Gail clutched her mug and Julia's hands covered hers. "I owe you big time."

"Yeah. You do."

Hawk was puzzled. As far as he knew, he'd never met Paul Benton. Yet the man seemed bent on seeing Hawk remain in jail. "Why would Paul Benton be working so hard against me?" he asked.

Julia and Gail just stared at him.

"I don't know," Julia finally answered.

"I do," Hawk said. "At least, I think I do. Maybe he's working for whoever is trying to keep Tierra Bonita from being rebuilt."

Julia and Gail both glanced over their shoulders as they mulled that over.

"Paul?" Julia said. "I can't believe it. Sure, he's a slime, but for him to stoop to being some sort of...mole? It's unfathomable."

Hawk was tense. Too tense to stay seated. He got up and started to pace around the kitchen. "Then give me another logic that works."

"I can't," Julia answered.

"Could he do this on his own?"

"Pu-lease," Gail said. "The man can't even open his own Outlook folder. I doubt that he's capable of master-minding an international escapade like this."

"I agree," Julia said.

"Then he's working for someone." Hawk moved behind Julia and placed his hands on her shoulders.

"The question is, for whom?" Julia turned to Gail. "Did Paul get all of your research?"

Gail grinned. "Yes, but I have copies. I emailed it all to myself before I hid the printed copy." She held up the papers she'd brought. "I printed them again at home."

Damn. Frustration welled up in Hawk and made standing still impossible, so he walked back and forth, wall to table. It didn't help. He needed a punching bag, or a long swim, or something. Anything to get rid of this feeling that something terrible was about to happen.

"What did you find?" Hawk asked Gail.

"A lot. And not enough at the same time." Gail handed the pages over to Julia. "First of all, Tierra Bonita is not a legal homestead according to the government. And I did find out that a U.S. company was recently deeded full land rights to the entire area."

"What?" Hawk's fists hit the table at the same time as the word reverberated off the kitchen walls.

"For the low, cool price of one million dollars."

Hawk's fists raised for another attack on the table.

"Hawk!" Julia snapped. "Can we focus here?"

He snapped his arms out, then clasped them behind his head. "What the hell is going on here?"

"I checked to see if anyone made inquiries into the land that Tierra Bonita sits on. International Law isn't my specialty, but I managed to get through to someone who disliked her boss enough to talk a bit. That's where I got the information. She wouldn't come right out and say it, but she implied that graft exchanged hands."

Both Hawk and Julia stared at her.

"Someone paid her boss to allow the bid for the land?"

Hawk felt like the floor had just disappeared. "Buy Tierra Bonita?"

"No. You misunderstand," Gail answered. "I don't think they are interested in the town. Just the land. The lady I spoke with said they didn't seem to care what was on the land."

Hawk felt Julia's hand on his, but shirked it off and grasped the kitchen counter. "Why the hell does someone want our land?"

"I don't know. I couldn't get that far in my search."

"Hawk, I've asked you before, but I'm going to ask again. Could someone in the village be behind this?"

He slapped the counter. "No way! It can't be someone from the village. They don't have the resources for this level of deception."

"Then who is doing this? Who wants this land? And why? Maybe that's the question we need to answer. Why would they want the land Tierra Bonita is built on?" Julia asked.

Hawk ran shaky hands through his hair. "I don't know."

"Are there any mineral rights?"

"No. I tried that when I was looking for financing to rebuild the village." He grimaced at how hard it had been to make that call. The idea of raping Tierra Bonita for minerals...

"A tactical advantage to where the village is situated?" Julia asked.

"Not that I can see," Hawk answered. "So, what else is there?"

After a moment, Julia spoke. "It's beautiful there."

"Yes," Hawk said, staring at her, knowing she was on the right track. "It's beautiful," he repeated. "A secluded cove and an ocean view. And hard to get to."

"Who would want that?"

"Celebrities," Gail said.

Hawk could almost see Julia's mind churning.

"A resort!" they said in unison.

"Someone wants to turn the village into a resort for the rich and famous," Hawk said.

"It makes sense," Julia answered.

He didn't hear her. The thought that someone would raze an entire town to build a fancy hiding place for people who could pay the right money was unbelievable.

"Who?" he asked.

Gail took the papers back from Julia. "The who is almost as hard as the why. Since she filed the paperwork, that disgruntled employee gave me a company name. Grandall Industries. I grabbed the thread and ran with it, but didn't get far. Grandall seems to be a shell company. They have a website that says they handle discreet real estate deals for, um, anonymous partners. Contact is by email only. No phone or address given. I tried to check into them further, but kind of hit a brick wall. If there's a chain to some sort of parent company, it's hidden deep." Gail picked up the second envelope. "Until someone approached me at a coffee shop yesterday and handed me this."

"Who?" Julia said.

"I have no clue. She was blonde, good-looking, and well dressed. Beyond that, she didn't give me a name or anything. She said, 'this will help' and was gone." She pulled the single page out and handed it to Julia.

Hawk leaned over Julia's shoulder, distracted for a moment by the fresh, slightly citrus scent to her hair. He inhaled deeply, wondering if they could go back to bed for a while.

Then, he saw the single name typed on the page Julia held and felt the kitchen spin out of control. He couldn't move a muscle as the colossal betrayal hit him like a wrecking ball.

He stared at the name.

H.K. Industries.

He knew it well. He flashed instantly back to a few years prior. His father, in a final bid to pull his errant son into the business, had created a company and handed it to Hawk on a silver platter. H.K. Industries.

Hawk had declined, and that final fight with his father had put the period on their relationship. He'd left Los Angeles that night with nothing but a gym bag of clothes, and except for the one other meeting in Tierra Bonita, they had not spoken since.

H.K. Industries. Could his father be the brains behind this fiasco? What had his father said on the yacht that night? *This village of yours is a shabby use of this prime space.*

Would his father do this? Hawk nodded. Yes. He now had absolutely no doubt. Why hadn't he seen it sooner? It was right up dear old Dad's sleeve. Cater to the rich and get richer. That was his motto. And how he lived his life.

Hawk couldn't breathe. He needed some space. He needed to get out of here. Looking around, he saw Julia and Gail staring at him.

"What?" he asked.

"You've been quiet."

"So?"

"Do you know this company?"

He prayed Julia would forgive him. "No. Never heard of them."

She squinted at him for a long while and finally let it drop.

"Okay," Julia said. "I think we need some time to digest this all. And I need a shower. Gail, do you want to stay?"

"As much as I'd like to, I have to get home to Pappy," she answered.

"Pappy," Julia said to Hawk, "is the schnauzer that allows Gail to occupy the same apartment."

"I think, now that I've given this"—Gail indicated the manila envelope— "to you, I can go in peace."

After seeing Gail out, Julia closed the door and thought about Hawk's reaction. He was holding out on her. She knew it like she knew how much he loved Tierra Bonita.

She walked back into the kitchen to find Hawk still sitting at the table, pouring over the paperwork Gail had left. He jumped when she touched his shoulder.

"You okay?" she asked.

"Sure. I'm just trying to figure this all out."

She waited for him to say more, but he clammed up. She had good intuition for who withheld information on the witness stand, and her instincts were screaming right now. Hawk was not telling her something. And there wasn't a damn thing she could do about it until he was ready to tell her. Stubborn fool.

"I'm going to take a shower."

"Okay," he said distractedly.

She watched him for a moment longer, then she headed to her bathroom.

When Julia came out a while later, papers were tossed all over the kitchen table and floor.

Hawk was gone.

CHAPTER THIRTEEN

A couple of hitched rides and here he was. Hawk stood in the plaza and stared at the skyscraper, an impressive tower of shadowed glass and burnished steel. The tallest building in town, it also boasted the highest lease fees. Hawk shook his head. He could still hear his father telling him that exact thing each time he walked into the old man's office.

"Boy, if you want to make money, you must exude money."

Disgust and an ultimatum had helped Hawk to finally say what was on his mind.

"I don't want this." He'd waved at Hakon Thoralssen I's office. "Any of it."

He'd walked out to the echo of barely concealed threats of denouncement and had never looked back. By the time he exited the skyscraper, he'd been grinning like a kid.

He wasn't smiling now. Rage smoldered in fists that shook like the ground in an earthquake. The fury traveled across clenched muscles to lodge like a brick in his heart. His own father was behind the village sabotage.

It would stop here and now. Hawk walked a measured pace across the plaza, entering the building that housed Thoralssen Industries. One way or the other, it would stop.

The elevator ride was interminable. Worse than waiting for that final leap onto a yacht they were about to steal. Much worse. Hawk looked down at his T-shirt and khaki shorts. He hadn't bothered to change and didn't much care. No one would stop him from getting to his father.

The doors opened, and Hawk entered the realm of Thoralssen Industries. He stopped to reconnoiter. It looked very much the same as it had when he'd last stormed out. Muted colors, modern furniture and expensive artwork conveyed affluence. He sniffed. The smell of paper, furniture polish and photocopiers seemed foreign to him. It had been a long, long time. Still, he felt an unfamiliar twinge. Had he missed this?

No.

He turned to the right without addressing the wide-eyed receptionist, and strode down the long hall to the executive suites.

"Excuse me," the voice behind him said.

He ignored it.

"Excuse me, sir." This time, a hand tried to latch onto his arm.

Hawk shook it off and kept walking. He heard the receptionist turn and run back toward her desk, but didn't care.

At the glass doors that signaled entrance to the executive suites, Hawk stopped to look at the numeric pad embedded in the wall. He punched in the old numbers from memory, and the doors opened with a *whoosh*.

Apparently, his father was capable of underestimating his own son. He'd never changed the access code.

Two women stood in his path, one blonde and one brunette, both obviously forewarned of his presence. He glared at them until the blonde raised her hands in submission and they moved out of his way.

He quickly reached his father's suite. The back of his neck prickled as the old dread returned. Hakon Thoralssen ran his empire from here. And his family, when they complied. Hawk believed to this day that his mother had died of a broken heart.

Squaring his shoulders, he opened the door to the inner sanctum. Not much had changed except maybe the material covering the chairs. But the leather couch, dark wood grains, and modern art work still looked the same. He saw the photograph of his mother. Not on the old man's desk, though. No. Hawk was certain his father wouldn't want to be reminded of what was good and decent in the world. He was too busy disintegrating it all in order to increase his empire.

The leather chair behind the desk was turned away from him.

"Hello, Dad," he said, forcing a composure he did not feel.

Hakon Thoralssen turned in his chair, appearing unsurprised at his son's entrance.

Hawk stood just inside the door and took stock of the man whose blood he shared. The same man who had wreaked havoc on Tierra Bonita. He hadn't aged a day in three years, still sporting a full head of white hair, the lean, muscled build of a much younger man, and piercing, ice-blue eyes.

Hakon got up from his stuffed leather chair and came around the desk, holding out a hand and smiling. "It's nice to see you finally come to your senses and come home."

"This isn't home, Dad. This is your office. Your day job. You never really could make that distinction, could you? My home is a small village called Tierra Bonita."

The old man's eyes narrowed.

"You know," Hawk continued, his voice dead calm, like the sniper who radios in that he's ready. "The one you've been trying to destroy?"

A commotion outside the office had them both turning their heads.

"You can't go in there!"

"Are you planning to stop me?"

Hawk recognized that don't-argue-with-me voice. To his dismay, his very indignant, auburn-headed counselor charged through the doors.

Julia had put two and two together quickly once she realized Hawk was gone. He knew the company listed on the sheet of paper Gail had been given by the blonde woman, which meant the company most likely belonged to Hawk's father. And that meant he was on his way to Los Angeles to confront the man.

Not bothering to change, she'd grabbed her car keys and purse and flown out the door. She'd hit the freeway a scant five minutes later, blue-tooth earbud firing away electronically for most of the drive to L.A.. Her first call was to Gail to grab the address for her and give her directions. Then, she began to systematically pull together the pieces of the puzzle in order to hand their evidence over to the authorities.

She'd made it to L.A. through midday traffic in just under two hours. It took another twenty minutes of frantic searching to find the building and park. She ran through the doors and wondered if Hawk had been through them already.

The turmoil as she exited the elevator answered her question.

Hawk was here.

"Which way to the executive offices?" Julia asked the woman standing in front of the reception desk.

The woman glanced down the hall. "You can't go down there."

Julia whirled and raced down the hall, through the open glass doors, stopping only to determine her new route. Angry voices came from the office to the left. Hawk's angry voice.

She headed in that direction only to have an arm restrain her. A blonde woman pulled her aside and spoke.

"You don't want to go in there, Julia."

Startled to hear herself named, Julia took a long look at the woman. "Do I know you?"

"No, but you will. For now, you'll have to trust that I'm on your side."

Julia shrugged off the arm and stared ice daggers at the woman. "Then you'd better follow me because you are not keeping me out."

The woman raised her hands once again. "Okay, just be careful. And be ready for anything. It's a powder keg in there."

"Don't I know it," Julia muttered as she ran forward into the office.

Hawk whirled on her. "Get out of here, Julia," he said through compressed lips. "This is my fight."

"You're wrong. It's our fight."

"He tried to destroy Tierra Bonita!"

"And my professional career," she shot back.

"I didn't destroy anything," the old man said calmly.

Both Hawk and Julia whipped around to face him. Julia got her first good look at Hawk's father and stuttered to a stop. Hakon Thoralssen I was not quite as tall as Hawk, but he was close. And those eyes! With the white hair, it was like looking into a mirror at Hawk's future.

"I saw Tierra Bonita for what it really is," Mr. Thoralssen continued. "And I intend to make it live up to its name. Beautiful land of God."

"You tried to wipe it out!" Hawk made as if to choke the man.

"I will make it better."

"By leveling an entire village?"

"Those people don't know what kind of gold mine they are sitting on. My God, son! Do you know what we can charge for the seclusion and view that area offers?"

"You've been planning this for some time." Hawk's voice was edged with defeat and Julia moved closer to him until he held up a hand to stop her.

"I already own the rights to the land. I just need those indigents to get the hell off and I can move forward."

"You sabotaged our efforts to restore basic needs."

"You gave me no choice," the elder Thoralssen said. "There was no way I could allow the village to be rebuilt. That mudslide was the best thing that's ever happened to the area. The plans are already drawn up. Let me show you." He moved toward a drafting table in the corner of his office.

Hawk stayed rooted in place. "Why, Dad? Why did you do it?"

Hakon Thoralssen I turned back and stared at his son. Julia knew the moment he realized there would be no converting Hawk. He straightened to his full height and returned Hawk's stare with obvious contempt. "Because I could," he said.

"My God, Dad. Tierra Bonita was Maria's home. Her family lives there. My family. That mudslide killed my wife!"

Hakon Thoralssen I snorted. "You're wife. I couldn't believe it when I heard you actually married that whore."

Julia saw Hawk's hands clench at his sides. This time she did move, putting herself between father and son.

"Hawk, stop. Don't listen to him. His opinion doesn't matter." She could see it wasn't working. Her argument fell on ears most likely pounding from a heart aching for vengeance.

Hawk was flushed red, but his eyes didn't waver from his father's face. "Take. It. Back."

"No." His father turned back to him. "That woman would have tainted our bloodline. You should never have married her. It's past time you took your place at my side and married someone who is of equal stature."

"You mean like when you married my mother?"

Hawk tried to step around Julia, but she was ready and moved with him. She was scared as hell, but ready. There was no way she would let him near his father with this much rage. It oozed out of every pore in his body. She could almost smell the sizzle of raw, burning emotion.

"You remember her, don't you?" Hawk said. "The woman who died of a broken heart when all she wanted was a little piece of yours?"

He tried again to move around her.

"Hawk." She tried to restrain him with an arm, but he threw it off. "Please. Don't do this."

"Stop right there, Hawk."

Julia turned to see who had interrupted them. The woman from the outer office stood behind Hawk with two other men, all with guns pointed directly at the man she loved. Fear clutched her throat like a noose, and her legs threatened to collapse her into a heap on the floor.

Hawk didn't turn. Hell, he didn't even acknowledge their presence. He continued to advance toward his father.

Julia maneuvered herself between Hawk and the guns. "No!" She cried. "Don't shoot. There's been no harm done."

The words finally penetrated Hawk's brain. Guns! And Julia stood between the guns and him. His chest constricted as he choked on the bile that clawed its way to release. *Please, God, no!* He whirled around, reached for Julia and yanked her behind him, his other hand up in the air as he yielded. "All right. I'll go peacefully," he said. "Leave Julia out of this."

The woman hesitated for only a moment, then holstered her pistol and moved toward them.

"There's been a lot of harm done," she said as she passed them and rounded the desk to the chalk-faced leader of Thoralssen Industries. He slumped to his chair.

"Hakon Thoralssen I, you are under arrest for bribery and an unlawful attempt to acquire domain land from a foreign country. And a few more items we're still working on arrest warrants for."

The two men with her handcuffed Hawk's father and read him his rights.

"You'll never make this stick," Hakon said, some of his old arrogance returning. "My lawyers will have me out by nightfall."

Hawk's mouth hung slack as his father was led away. He couldn't quite wrap his mind around everything that had happened. It was over. His father would pay for his sins. More importantly, the village and Julia were now safe from harm.

"Ouch. Hawk, let me go," Julia said. "You're squeezing me too hard."

"Oh, um, sorry," he said as he loosened his hold. What he really wanted to do was roar. He felt like he'd just run a marathon...or captured a yacht. It was over too soon and there was no outlet for the adrenaline rush that flooded his body.

He turned to Julia.

Fascinated by the wild excitement in Hawk's eyes, Julia knew this must be what he looked like as he overtook yachts. No wonder people wanted revenge. With those intense eyes and his hair untied, he must have scared the wits out of them.

The blonde stuck out her hand. "Kate Milden, F.B.I., at your service."

Julia shook it, then pointed to the door in confusion. "You were outside."

"Yes, I tried to stop you." She shook her head. "You're a stubborn woman."

Hawk pulled Julia against him and chuckled. "Don't I know it?"

"I was undercover," Kate said. "We knew Thoralssen played dirty. When he wanted something, he stopped at nothing to get it."

Hawk stiffened and Julia watched the blood drain from his face, so she tucked an arm around him and asked the question she knew he wanted to. "What do you mean anything?"

"Not murder. Not much short of that, in some cases, but he never got to the point where he crossed that line."

Julia felt Hawk's muscles ease as Kate continued.

"Like I said, he went beyond the bounds of the law in a lot of cases to get what he wanted. However, Thoralssen Industries is just too big, too powerful. We couldn't get enough to indict him, which is where I came in. I never told my family about my real job. They think I travel to purchase art for a local gallery. So when I took the job as Mr. Thoralssen's assistant, he had no reason to suspect I was anything more than what my resume said. Working for him gave me an opportunity to gather intel."

"Wait a minute," Hawk said. "I know you. My father tried to set us up at one point, didn't he?"

Julia's eyes narrowed. This was someone from Hawk's life before Mexico? She took a closer look at the woman. Blonde hair, blue eyes, and curvy in all the right places. Kate Milden was beautiful. Too beautiful. Wondering if their prior relationship had been all that innocent, she tried to pull away from Hawk.

He only pulled her in tighter. "Put your claws away, my love. We never even dated," he said, kissing the top of her head. "Our families ran in the same circles. That's all."

It was enough to make Julia relax, and she snuggled deeper.

"Yes," Kate said with a glance at Julia. "Sorry, Hawk, but you're not my type. I like 'em weak and malleable." She chuckled. "At least, for now, that's what works."

Julia's head whipped up. "You gave the envelope to Gail!"

Kate nodded. "We were close to indicting Mr. Thoralssen, but needed to force the issue. Sorry, Hawk. The friction between you and your father seemed the perfect ploy to, um, encourage him to slip and incriminate himself."

Hawk ran his free hand through his hair. "What's going to happen to him?"

"We hope he's held without bail. Our case is solid, and the charges are serious enough to warrant that. And he's got enough money to be considered a flight risk." Kate took a deep breath. "It is my belief that he will spend the rest of his life in jail."

Julia watched the furrow between Hawk's eyes deepen. She reached up and touched his face so he would look at her. "He's still your father."

"Yeah. At one time, we actually had some affection for each other."

"I'm sorry."

"So am I." He squared his shoulders. "He's the one who walked down this path. I don't regret having a part in stopping his activities."

"And you've got a lot of family to lean on in Tierra Bonita."

"Yes." He smiled.

"And me."

"Thank God." He kissed her, leaving no doubt of his love.

Kate cleared her throat. "Um, there's one more thing I need to come clean about."

Grinning, Julia asked what it was.

Kate pulled papers out of her back pocket and handed them to her. The heading said, *Sure Deal Bail Bonds*.

"You!"

"Yes," Kate said, scrunching her face.

"What?" Hawk asked.

Julia handed him the papers. "You posted Hawk's bail?"

"I'm sorry. I hated to do that, but my superiors wanted him out of jail."

"Why did you have to use my name?"

"I needed you both distracted until we were ready."

"Do you have any idea how much trouble you have caused for me? I could be disbarred."

"Don't worry. We'll call Stanski, Rawlins, & Benton and let them know it wasn't you. We'll also inform them you were involved in an F.B.I. investigation and couldn't discuss it."

Julia was still huffing. "You'd better. I know a damn good attorney."

"So do I," Hawk said. "So do I."

Kate sobered. "That's good, because we still have one issue to resolve. What are we going to do with you?"

Her radio crackled, and she walked a few steps away to respond.

Julia kissed Hawk, afraid that, if he went back in jail, there wouldn't be much more in the way of opportunity. At least, not for a while.

"For now," Kate said, rejoining them, "we'll have to turn you over to the local authorities. You did jump bail and leave the country, after all."

"That I did," Hawk said with a sigh.

Kate smiled, glancing from one to the other. "Looks like it's a good thing you've got yourself a great attorney, then."

"Do we have to call the police?" Julia asked.

"No. With my partners gone, I can drop you at the station."

Julia looked at Hawk. "Um," she said to Kate, "could we have a moment alone, please?"

"I think we can manage that." Kate went out to reception, pulling the door closed behind her.

Julia wasted no time, turning into Hawk's embrace and clinging to him. His arms tightened to just short of a vise, and he leaned his head forward to inhale her scent.

She reached for his neck and pulled him down into a long, slow, sensual kiss. She needed to remember the feel of his lips on hers.

Hawk groaned and deepened the kiss. Hands that held her began to move along her body, to soothe her, to awaken the fire in her. He cupped her breast through her clothing, and his thumb traced a gentle line across her nipple, which sent shivers of desire coursing through her. Again, he caressed her and the tremors amplified.

She arched her back, bringing her in tighter contact with his erection and giving him greater access to her breasts. He slid a hand under her sweater, around her back, and deftly unhooked her bra. Then, he lifted the impeding clothing up and lowered his head, taking a taut tip into his mouth.

"Oh!" Julia sighed and ground her hip into him as he played with her. His free hand caressed her hips and nudged her legs apart. Even through her slacks, his touch could send her over the top.

Hawk shifted and stared into her eyes. Then, he lifted her and moved to the sofa.

"Hawk, we can't. Someone could walk in."

"No one will," he said, undoing her zipper and slipping her jeans down. His attention returned to her breast, and he surrounded it with kisses, sucking the nipple into his mouth as his hand wandered a path down her stomach and lower.

Hawk moved as if they had all the time in the world, stroking back and forth until Julia thought she would scream. She grabbed his head, intent on pulling him to her, but he settled between her legs and replaced his fingers with his mouth.

It was heaven. And hell. The sensations washed over Julia until she was swept away on a final wave of climax.

Hawk held her until the feeling subsided.

Julia tried to pull him to her, but he resisted. "Not this time, sweetheart. This one is to remember me by." He smiled tenderly at her.

"You're tough to forget," she said as she moved her hands over his face. "I love you, pirate."

He smiled. "I could not live without you, my love. You have my heart for all time."

"And you, mine."

"For now, though, we'd probably better get you dressed."

Julia straightened her clothes and turned worried eyes on Hawk, who had moved to stare out the window. "How are we going to get you out of jail?"

"I don't know, counselor." He motioned for her to join him and enfolded her in his arms with a smile. "But I have every confidence that my attorney will find a way. I trust her with my life."

Julia bit her bottom lip to keep from reminding him she had not been very successful originally.

Julia and Hawk walked arm in arm out of the office.

Kate turned to them, her face a mask of sadness. "I'm so sorry," she said.

Hawk knew what she would say. It settled in the roiling pit of his stomach and the utter calm of his heart. "What?" he asked, merely as a formality.

"It's your father. He never made it to the jail. It looks like his heart…"

"He's dead." Hawk finished.

"Yes."

Funny. He should feel something, shouldn't he? Two hours ago, he'd wanted to kill the old man himself. There should be some pleasure. Some remorse. Something besides an utter numbness.

He felt a hand on his arm. Julia's.

His father was dead. He tried the words out in his mind to see if they would evoke a response. Nothing. Not a damn tear or a single regret. So this would be his father's epitaph. To have lived according to his own needs and have no one to mourn him in the end.

What a waste.

Hawk put his arm around Julia. "I'm okay," he whispered. Turning to Kate, he simply said, "I'm ready to go."

CHAPTER FOURTEEN

Julia sat in her car, in front of San Diego County Jail, and wondered, once again, how she would break the news to Hawk. Leaning her head on hands that gripped the steering wheel, she dreaded the confrontation.

He wasn't going to like it. Not one bit.

She sat up, took a deep breath, and opened her car door. It was time to get it over with.

Inside, Julia endured county lock-up procedures, then the *whoosh, clank* of the jail doors opening.

She sat for interminable minutes in the attorney/client room before they ushered Hawk in. Julia smiled. He looked awfully damn good, even after an agonizing month in jail. He hadn't shaved in a couple days, and the rugged stubble only made her want him more. His blond mane was getting scrubby and needed a trim. She imagined running her fingers through the strands. He could cut it maybe. But not too much.

Hawk stood just inside the door, afraid the mirage would disappear. He had dreamt of her so often in this hellhole that he couldn't be certain she was real.

"Hello," she said in that low, sexy voice he'd heard echoing through his mind ever since being locked up.

Each time she came to visit him, she seemed more beautiful. Her hair was down today, not in its usual clip. A familiar stirring struck him full in the groin. God, he needed to get out of here and make love to her. Visions of her pervaded his days and haunted his nights.

Hawk sat down and placed his hands palm down on the table as if making an impression in cement. If he didn't do this carefully, he would jump over the table and take her here and now.

Julia covered his hands with hers, and he shivered with need. "Easy, guy. This isn't a conjugal visit."

Just the possibility made him hard. "Do they allow that here?"

Julia laughed, and the sound eased the pain in his groin. "Sorry. You'd have to go to the state pen to even be able to petition for that."

"Well, then..." His eyes gleamed with anticipation.

Julia's tone turned serious. "You're not going to get that far."

Hope rekindled. "You have news."

Tapping her fingers on the table, she answered, "Yes."

Hawk waited long seconds before she continued.

"You're not going to like it."

"Out with your news, woman," he growled.

"Well, you remember telling me that your Dad disowned you?"

Hawk frowned. "Yes."

"If he did," Julia said, "he forgot to make it official. You were never written out of his will. As it turns out, you're the only heir."

The words didn't sink in. Heir? Heir to what?

"Hawk, your father's companies, his properties, his resources. Everything he amassed—it's all yours."

"You're kidding me."

"Nope."

His father's money. Money earned through the sweat and blood of others. Tainted money. He leaned back and laced his fingers behind his head for a long moment, then shook his head. "I don't want it."

"Hawk—"

He slammed his fists on the table, causing Julia to jump and the guard to open the door. She waved the guard away and waited for Hawk to continue.

"No. I don't want a damn cent. He stole his money by shredding other people's lives. Honest, hard-working people. I won't take a dime of it."

"Hawk, think for a minute. Think about the good you could do with the money. You could wipe out a lot of the harm your father did."

"I don't want to absolve him. I hope he rots in hell!"

But the thought stuck. It prickled his brain and wound its way through his body until his heart joined the conversation. With that kind of money, Hawk could accomplish a lot. He could... Hawk rubbed his chin. He could finish the village work.

Massaging his forehead, he felt the burden he had carried ever since Maria's death lift. Her home would be restored. He would keep his promise to her.

When he lifted his head, he knew tears filled his eyes. He swallowed them back, noticing a wary caution on Julia's face. Breathing deeply, he asked for the rest of the information she was here to tell him. "What's the downside, counselor?"

"What makes you think there's a downside?"

"Because I know you better than I know myself," he said softly. "There's something you don't want to tell me."

"I rather thought telling you about the money would be bad enough. But there is one more thing. I, um, brokered a deal without your knowledge."

He shrugged. "Okay."

"Okay? That's it?"

"Yes. I trust you." The way she fidgeted with the papers in front of her had him rethinking things. "Shouldn't I?"

"Of course. I'm just not sure how to tell you exactly what I did."

He covered her hands with his own, and she took a deep breath. "Since you now have these almost unlimited resources at your disposal, I took the liberty of contacting the insurance companies who want you prosecuted."

"And?"

"And I asked them if they would drop the charges if you paid complete recompense for their time and efforts."

"That doesn't sound too bad."

"Plus a little bit more for punitive damages."

"Just how much more?"

Julia scrunched her face and leaned over, whispering the amount into his ear.

"What?" His voice boomed and the guard scowled in his direction.

"Hawk—"

"Woman, that's a hell of a lot of money."

"Yes, but it's a pittance compared to the worth of Thoralssen Industries."

"Seriously?"

"Yes."

"So...did they agree?"

Julia cocked an eyebrow and grinned. "Yes."

"And the yacht owners?"

"Don't care. They've been paid by the insurance companies and are already sailing their new acquisitions. Well, I did offer them a little money just to make sure they'd stay happy. Small stuff compared to the insurance companies."

Hawk blew out a long breath. "So, I'm free?"

"It looks that way."

A decidedly devilish gleam entered his eyes. "When?"

"We still need to get the judge to sign off on it."

Hawk gripped her hands. "When?"

"A few days. Maybe a week."

"I don't think I can wait that long."

"Well, you'd better."

"Today, Tierra Bonita del Dios becomes a village of the people, owned by the people." He pulled the cover off the plaque that had been placed on the main hall and translated it into English.

In honor of Maria Thoralssen.

Daughter, Sister, Wife, and Friend.

Live, Laugh, Love.

"Daughter"—he glanced at Manuel and Mama Rosa, — "wife"—he looked over the villagers gathered here— "and friend to all. Maria would be very proud of what we have accomplished here, even with"—Hawk coughed— "the somewhat unorthodox means we employed."

Julia said a quiet prayer of thanks to those "unorthodox means" as a collective chuckle rolled through the group. If it hadn't been for those methods she might never have met Hakon Thoralssen II. She might never have had the opportunity to fall in love with the people of Tierra Bonita. She might never have known what it was like to love a man who believed and trusted in her so much, he'd gone back to jail, never doubting that she would find a way to free him.

"Bienvenido a casa. Welcome home," Hawk finished.

A ribbon had been placed across the entrance to the main hall, and Mama Rosa cut it, officially announcing that it was time to celebrate. Cheers broke out as everyone poured into the building and began to roll food and drink out for the celebration.

Julia and her mother waited near the hall for Hawk to join them. When he finally did, he first bent down to kiss Helen Branholt's cheek. Julia was astounded to see a blush color her mother's pale face as Hawk straightened. "Trying to get on your mother-in-law's good side, Mr. Thoralssen?"

"You bet, Mrs. Thoralssen," he said, grinning.

Helen Branholt waved a gloved hand in the air. "You had my vote the minute you asked to marry my daughter. Even before that, if I may be so bold. I recognized the look on her face right after she met you."

"Really?" Hawk's eyes sparkled as he pulled Julia into his arms. "You were attracted to me that quickly?"

"You were just another pro bono case dumped in my lap," Julia said. "Right up until I saw you. I knew then my life was forever changed."

"For the better, I hope."

"For the best." She snuggled in closer.

Mama Rosa came through the doors. "Asi, Asi. Come. It is time to celebrate." She propelled Helen's wheelchair into the hall, not waiting for Hawk and Julia.

"I still can't believe my mother is here," Julia said.

"Why shouldn't she be here?"

"Because it's so hard for her." Julia said, a frown deeply seated in her brow. "The multiple sclerosis is taking her so fast."

"Her doctor cleared her, and she is more than capable of making this trip." He hugged Julia tighter. "With luck, it will not be her time for many years. I admire her independent spirit. And that she passed it on to her daughter."

Julia took a deep breath and tried to convince herself that what Hawk said was true. She prayed there would be many more days, years even, with her mother.

Julia moved over to the plaque and ran her hands across it.

"That was a nice touch," Hawk said. "You didn't have to have it made."

"It seemed appropriate. I owe Maria a lot."

"What—"

"She showed you that not everyone is like your father. She showed you what love is. She gave you hope. And you, in turn, showed me how to love."

Hawk nodded his head, then reached for Julia's hand and planted a kiss on the inside of her wrist that sent quivers straight to her heart. "Come on." He cocked his head to the doors. "It's time to celebrate."

The hall was noisier than when she'd first arrived in this village, if that was even possible. This time, though, Julia didn't balk. This time, the noise welcomed her home.

Dion waved them over, and they joined them at the table. Julia hugged Claire carefully and took a moment to peek inside the native sling that held little Joseph. "He's adorable, Claire."

Claire beamed. "He is, isn't he?" She glanced at her son. "I am worried about all this noise, though. He's only four weeks old, after all."

"I think," Dion said, "if it bothered him, he would be telling us rather raucously instead of sleeping so peacefully."

"He does have a way of letting us know when he is unhappy."

Hawk clapped Dion on the shoulders. "Congratulations, man. He's a handsome boy."

"Thanks. The birth was a rough go there for a while."

Claire laughed. "My tough, ex-agent husband had a rougher time than Joseph and I did, I think. He was so distraught that Manuel and the men had to pull him away and ply him with drink."

Dion grinned. "I didn't stay away long."

"No. You came back and saw it through." Her eyes shone with a bond that only two in love could know.

"He never could hold his liquor." Julia turned to the new voice. It belonged to a man with brown hair styled in a trendy, over the eye cut. Devilish green eyes twinkled as he spoke. "Aidan Walker, at your service." He executed a formal bow in front of her.

Hawk whispered in her ear. "He was Dion's partner and helped to capture me."

Julia turned back to Aidan. "Well, then, I guess I should thank you. Without you"—she turned to Dion— "and you, I would never have met my husband."

"Then we have much to celebrate," Aidan said, plopping down next to Gail. Julia's friend had arrived late this afternoon with Julia's mother.

Hawk offered the seat next to Gail to his Julia.

"What?" Gail said to Hawk. "You're not afraid of me, are you?"

"Woman, you almost gelded me. I'm not giving you another shot at it."

"Don't mess with my boss and you won't have to worry," Gail said.

"Who is your boss?" Aidan asked as he settled in beside her.

"Julia. Well, actually, Thoralssen Industries."

Aidan glanced around her at Julia. "You are running the Thoralssen empire?"

"Hardly," Julia answered. "It turns out that Hawk"—she jabbed her husband in the ribs— "has a talent for running multi-billion-dollar businesses. He's in the process of turning Thoralssen Industries into something more...palatable."

Hawk grimaced.

"I handle the legal end of things. And I couldn't do it without Gail."

Gail nodded impishly. "She's right. I'm irresistible. I mean, irreplaceable," she giggled.

Aidan leaned over and whispered something in her ear, which had Julia staring at them wide-eyed. She turned to Dion, who shrugged.

Dion looked at Hawk. "Well said out there, my friend. Well said."

"Thank you." Hawk looked over the room. "It's really done, isn't it?"

"Yes." Dion laughed. "The trust is set up to self-perpetuate, thanks to your generous funding."

"And the deed has been signed over to the village," Hawk said, "so there will be no more attempts to seize this land."

Helen Branholt arrived then, pushed by Mama Rosa, with a tray of glasses and a pitcher of juice seated on her lap. "It would be a shame for such a lovely place to be spoiled by commercialization."

"That will never happen again," Hawk said.

"Thank goodness."

After a meal filled with local favorites, the group sat drinking strong coffee.

"What will you and Claire do now?" Hawk asked Dion.

"This will always feel like home to us," Claire answered. "But Dion's been offered a position with the Gates Foundation."

Cheers lit the table up for a long moment.

"Impressive," Julia said.

"Yes. We may be moving to Seattle." Claire nudged her husband. "First, though, we're going to travel up to San Diego. Dion here promised to show me Hawaii, but I think it will have to wait until Joseph is a little older."

Aidan pulled his attention away from Gail long enough to ask a question. "Whatever happened to that guy you worked with? You know, the one who was on Thoralssen's payroll?"

"Paul Benton?" Julia grimaced. "He's no longer part of Stanski, Rawlins, and Benton, that's for sure. Last I heard, he was waiting for the review board to determine if he could still practice law." Her eyes clouded over. "I gave a deposition. I hope he's denied renewal of his license." She brightened then. "Did I tell you that I was offered partner?"

"No!" Claire said.

"Yes. Stanski, Rawlins, and Thoralssen. I guess they liked the idea of that name on the door. Turning them down was one of the highlights of my year."

"So, you'll be calling San Diego home permanently then?" Dion asked.

Julia shook her head. "San Diego is where we live. I think, though"—she gazed up at her husband— "that Tierra Bonita will always be our home."

Later, Julia excused herself from the festivities to wander down to the beach. Staring at the silver moonlight on the water, she thought of the picture in her office. Her father had received so many accolades in his life. How many times growing up had she heard someone talk about the law being in his blood? She believed it. She had no clue if he had ever loved anything except the next case. She hugged herself as the sadness of what he missed out on washed through her.

The law was in her blood, too. She'd proven that. There were things that mattered more, though. Love mattered more.

"I just won the case of a lifetime, Dad." Julia looked up at the night sky. "I won the heart of my pirate. And that's all the success I need."

Steady arms surrounded her. "And you did it before your thirtieth birthday."

Julia turned in the arms of her friend, her lover, her husband. "I wasted so much time trying to be something I didn't want to be."

"It wasn't a waste. If it hadn't been for your drive to succeed, I would have never met you, never gotten a chance to know the tiger within you. And I would never have reached this level of happiness without you."

"I love you forever," she said.

"Promise?"

"Always."

EPILOGUE

A few days later, Julia lounged on the patio of their new home in Chula Vista. Hawk joined her, wine glasses and a nice merlot in hand. After a leisurely kiss, he opened the bottle.

"None for me, thank you," Julia said with a gleam in her eye as she watched him.

He stopped mid-pour. "Are you all right?"

"Yes," she answered with a smile. "We are."

It took a few seconds before his face registered understanding. Hawk set the wine down and, grinning broadly, knelt on one leg by her chair. He placed one of those massive hands on her stomach as if it was the most precious thing in the world. Then, he looked up at her and she saw the awe in his face, certain it was mirrored in her own.

"I only just found out this afternoon," she said, her hand brushing his cheek.

"We were in meetings together all day. How—"

"It only takes five minutes in a bathroom to know for sure these days."

"Why didn't you tell me?"

Julia placed a finger over his lips, temporarily mesmerized at how familiar and sensual they felt. She smiled. "Because this has nothing to do with business. I wanted us to be here." She gazed out at the sea. "At home. Just the three of us."

Hawk smiled and kissed her tenderly.

"You know, if I'm right, this baby was conceived on one of our jaunts to Tierra Bonita."

His smile broadened.

"Promise me that our child will know where his roots are."

"His?"

Julia shrugged her shoulders. "Just a hunch."

Hawk gathered Julia in his arms and, together, they gazed out at the ocean. "I promise."

Thank you for reading **Pirate's Promise, book 2 of the Tropical Persuasions series.** If you enjoyed this book, please consider leaving an honest review wherever you prefer, and know that it would be greatly appreciated.

And be sure to check out Aidan and Gail's story in **Dare To Love,** the exciting conclusion to this series.

For new release information and news about Laurie Ryan, please sign up for her newsletter at www.laurieryanauthor.com.

BOOKS BY LAURIE RYAN

Contemporary Romance stories

<u>Billionaire Bachelor Pledge series</u>

Royal Flush

High Card

All In

Full House

Blind Bet

<u>Willow Bay series</u>

Last Resort

Finding Home

Chances Are

Tender Tide

Reluctant Christmas

Operation Ethan

<u>Tropical Persuasions series</u>

Stolen Treasures

Pirate's Promise

Dare to Love

Standalone

The Long Journey Home

Rudy's Heart

Lost and Found

Northern Lights

Healing Love

Women's Fiction

Show Me

Fantasy

Survival

Enlightenment

Birthright

Awakening

Wolf's Call

ABOUT THE AUTHOR

Laurie Ryan writes about resilient, independent women who might stumble, but they dust themselves off and get the job done. Their men, whether commanding alpha or endearing cinnamon roll heroes, will do whatever it takes to ensure the happiness of the women they cherish.

Laurie lives in the Pacific Northwest with her "he can fix anything" hubby, but is always willing to travel to visit their children and grandchildren. Her creativity isn't limited to writing. She also scrap books and, when she really needs to disappear, she paints rocks and shells found on the beaches she walks at the ocean—her happy place.

Laurie has always had a deep connection to nature and the outdoors, which is reflected in her writing. She is a passionate writer who brings her love for nature, animals, and creativity into her work.

An avid cruiser, Laurie has visited many places. One of her favorites was a stop in Greenland, where the strength and endurance of the people living in those beautiful but harsh surroundings became an underlying thread in her stories. Her sensual romance novels are sure to warm the hearts of readers.

Connect with Laurie on Facebook, Instagram, or TikTok, or her website, and join Laurie's newsletter for up to date news and releases.

Laurie loves to hear from her readers and can be reached at laurie@laurieryanauthor.com

SNEAK PREVIEW

Dare To Love

(book three in the Tropical Persuasions series)
By Laurie Ryan

The Story

Sometimes the greatest risk is daring to love.

Dare to trust...

Gail Grayson thought she'd finally found her happily-ever-after—until the man who stole her heart vanished without a trace. Now Aidan Walker is back, more dangerous and magnetic than ever, stirring up old wounds and impossible hopes. One look into those storm-tossed eyes and her battered heart starts to whisper... *what if?*

Dare to believe...

Maritime piracy operative Aidan Walker lives by one rule:

never stay, never need, never love. Walking away keeps him safe—because everyone leaves eventually. But Gail is different. Fierce. Unforgettable. The one woman who makes him question the walls he's spent a lifetime building. This time, he's not sure he can let her go... or survive if she lets *him* go.

Dare to love...

With a ruthless cartel closing in and fate throwing every obstacle in their path, Aidan and Gail must decide if love is worth the risk. In a world where loyalty is a liability and every choice could cost them everything, can they find the courage to trust, to believe... and to dare forever?

SNEAK PEEK

Chapter One

Prologue

"What do you say we blow this party, find some nice, quiet, uninhabited place, and get to know each other a whole lot better?"

Gail Grayson rolled her eyes, even as her ears tingled at the whispered words. That tingle wound its way past her brain as Aidan Walker settled an arm across the back of her chair.

She'd come to Mexico to help friends celebrate the renovation of a local village. Now, with the dedication behind them, the brightly painted gathering hall was overflowing with locals and visitors all bent on laughter and fun. Two hours ago, Gail had watched Aidan walk into the party like a predatory animal. He'd commandeered the seat next to her and hadn't left. Apparently, the man had trained his sights on her.

Don't think, her mind taunted in response to his question. *Just go. Be with him.*

It was hard to say no when she took time to appreciate the man whose hand traced the curves of her forearm. Brown hair, cut in a trendy, over-the-eye style, couldn't quite hide the Irish in his green eyes. His lips quirked with mischief while he waited for her acceptance.

Gail's heart joined the chorus, its beat picking up with each slow, tortuous stroke of his hand along her arm.

She wanted to go with him. Lord, how she wanted to. Gail watched as his finger wound a lazy trail back and forth, and she almost gave in to the hunger that had her ready to explode.

Wide, muscled shoulders and a trim waist only added to the effect he had on her. Aidan Walker was hot. Not just hot, he was tossing flames that threatened to engulf her.

Gail resisted the urge to fan herself, but she made the fatal mistake of looking into his eyes. Little lines crinkled at the corners as he watched her, then he raised an eyebrow in challenge.

He knew how her mind was ogling him.

Damn it. This was not how things worked. She always had the upper hand when it came to flirting. Always. This seduction had gone on quite long enough and it was time to take back control.

Resting an elbow on the table, Gail cupped her chin and leaned closer to Aidan. She used her tongue to moisten lips she knew were colored the perfect shade of red and was satisfied to see his eyes dip to follow the movement.

"Isn't that what we're doing?" she asked.

"Huh?" A hint of confusion in his eyes was the only indication she got, but Gail knew she had re-taken the lead.

"I said,"—she paused, giving him time to focus— "isn't that what we're doing? Getting to *know* each other?" She used the hushed, sensual tone of her voice like a spell and Aidan's green eyes flared with a very gratifying desire as he responded.

"Not even close, darlin'."

Gail allowed her lips to curve into a lazy smile, even as her heart raced. "What would you call it then?"

Aidan's breath fluttered the short hair around her ear as he leaned in. "Foreplay." The word rolled off his tongue like melted chocolate. Deep, dark, and sinful.

Gail craved that bite of chocolate so badly she found it hard to breathe. Sitting back, she ran shaky fingers through her short hair and drew a slow breath.

Round one to you, Aidan Walker.

***

More information about this story and more by Laurie Ryan can be found on her website.

www.ingramcontent.com/pod-product-compliance
Lightning Source LLC
Chambersburg PA
CBHW060349310726
48976CB00003B/766